Suppose The Wolf Were An Octopus

Grades 3 to 4

A Guide To Creative Questioning for Elementary Grade Literature

by

Michael T. Bagley, Ed.D.

Third Printing

Trillium Press

Monroe, New York
Toronto, Ontario

Trillium Press   **Trillium Press**
PO Box 209   203 College St., Suite 200
Monroe, N.Y. 10950   Toronto, Ontario
(914) 783-2999   M5T 1P9 Canada
FAX: (914) 782-6359

ISBN: 0-89824-096-4
Printed in the United States of America by the Royal Fireworks Press
of Monroe, N.Y.

Table of Contents

SPECIFIC PURPOSES OF THE BOOK

1. To demonstrate the procedure for building different levels of questions from children's literature.

2. To encourage teachers to develop questions from all instructional areas.

3. To encourage teachers to use multi-level questions in group discussions.

4. To demonstrate that higher level thinking can be attained through effective questioning.

5. To demonstrate that primary grade literature has the potential to arouse stimulating questions.

6. To provide a number of stories from primary literature, so that a range of subjects and topics are available to teachers.

7. To provide examples of questions at different cognitive levels.

8. To provide several strategies for questioning in the teaching/learning process.

QUESTIONING IN THE INSTRUCTIONAL PROCESS

"In every age, in every society, there is always one who wonders, one who questions."

Eileen Lynch

Imagination can be enhanced only when one is given the opportunity to play with ideas, to discover relationships, and, most important, to ask questions. If, as educators, we demonstrate to the child that his/her ideas have value and his/her questions will be listened to, we are adding a rich source of fuel to that child's motivation for learning. It seems that involving students in higher level questioning will subsequently lead to a more open-minded, self-confident, inquiring person. It is our contention that teachers who actively engage in asking higher level questions will stimulate and increase the amount of child-initiated questions with teachers, family and peers.

Hypothesis No. 1

Teachers who show an appreciation for questioning, who establish a climate where diverse questions are valued, who consistently ask high quality questions will develop students who demonstrate greater involvement in the questioning process.

Students who are encouraged to ask questions are being given an opportunity to explore with their minds, to gain meaning for themselves and to relate new data with old concepts. The new questions, new theories and new ideas remain the most important part of the learning process.

Another benefit in using higher level questions is that it can provide an open-ended learning situation. When one seeks to ask questions about things or events that have no one right answer or a multitude of potentially right answers, an attitude develops where one appreciates the immensity and complexity of the real world data. Perhaps this point can be illustrated by the following quotation:

"Just when I knew all of life's answers, they changed all the questions."

Hallmark Card, Inc.

It is our belief that a classroom situation where questioning is held in high regard will result in an environment that is healthier, and one in which students are more receptive.

Hypothesis No. 2

Teachers who use higher level questions on a consistent basis will increase their students' higher level thinking skills in terms of frequency, depth, appropriateness and complexity.

This second hypothesis involves a concept which is paramount to our beliefs and practices. It is a relationship between good question asking and diverse thinking experiences. One of the basic goals in education is to provide opportunities which will stimulate the learners' higher level thinking skills. A method conducive to enhancing the students' thinking skills is an inquiry-based approach to learning.

QUESTIONING. . .THE BASIS OF INQUIRY

Inquiry is defined by J. Richard Suchman (1968) as a fundamental and natural process of learning by which an individual gathers information, raises and tests hypotheses, builds theories, and tests them empirically. If we relate questioning to this definition, several points can be made.

First, we feel that questioning is a natural process fueled by curiosity—a basic human characteristic. Second, in order to collect data, we must ask questions about the different sources, types and significance of that data. Third, when one begins to develop his/her own theories, we can assume that this person went through the process of question-asking; and, finally, one of the basic findings or conclusions usually generated from rigorous investigation is the development of new, unanswered questions.

If we believe that inquiry is a necessary condition for independence and autonomy of learning, then we must give serious attention to the role of questioning in the teaching/learning process. We have taken Suchman's three concepts and related them to the questioning process.

Freedom

The more rules and restrictions thrown in the way of the child, the less chance he/she has for asking questions or responding to the questions of others. A part of freedom is autonomy and an autonomous learner will undoubtedly question.

Responsiveness

The child who questions must have a rich supply of data available when he or she wants it. Children who question freely and have access to a responsive statement are bound to come up with formulations that represent the way that child sees and attempts to account for the phenomena of his/her world.

Focus

Questioning is most productive when it has direction and purpose. It is the teacher's role to guide and assist the learner in focusing on relevant topics and issues, or as Suchman emphasizes, "discrepant events." These are events that present a phenomena that does not coincide with the child's knowledge and understanding of the world. A gap is created between what the child perceives and what he/she knows.

It is the teacher's responsibility to maintain the conditions of freedom, responsiveness and focus.

THE CLIMATE FOR QUESTIONING

In order for questioning to take place, the climate of the classroom must be conducive. This climate does not happen by accident, and creating it requires a conscious effort on the part of the teacher. A classroom that is full of excitement, a sense of wonder, and an openness to ideas, where there is thoughtful consideration of data, a willingness to take risks, and a lack of concern over personal achievement—this is where questioning will take place. A classroom characterized by an authoritative text and an equally authoritarian teacher stifles questioning.

The teacher can shape the classroom climate. If he/she provides psychological space for students to ask divergent questions without fear of failure or embarrassment, the proper climate is likely to develop.

A climate that encourages students to think and question beyond the scope of the curriculum will yield greater student productivity and a more exciting learning environment. In recognizing the importance of establishing a climate which rewards divergent thinking, Torrance, P. (1963) suggests that teachers respond to students in the following ways: a) Treat unusual questions with respect; b) Treat unusual ideas with respect; b) Provide opportunities for self-initiated learning; d) Show children that their ideas have value; e) Provide periods of non-evaluative practice or learning.

Students who are exposed to this type of learning environment will gain confidence in themselves as autonomous learners. If the teacher is always didactic and restrictive or if he/she plays the role of the ultimate authority in the classroom, the students will develop a dependency on the teacher in an effort to play his/her game and receive the rewards offered.

Reason can answer questions, but imagination has to ask them!

Ralph W. Gerard

BLOOM'S TAXONOMY OF EDUCATIONAL OBJECTIVES

The basic framework for this text comes from the work of Benjamin Bloom (1956), who created the classification of educational objectives in a book called *Taxonomy of Educational Objectives*. In his book, Bloom presents six major cognitive operations: Knowledge, Comprehension, Application, Analysis, Synthesis, and Evaluation. In order to better understand these constructs, we have presented a brief description below of each classification.

Level	Description
L-1 Knowledge	These are questions that check the basic facts about people, places or things (information gathering).
L-2 Comprehension	These are questions that check your understanding and memory of facts (confirming).
L-3 Application	Application questions test your ability to use your knowledge in a problem-solving, practical manner (illuminating).
L-4 Analysis	These are questions in which we select, examine and break apart information into its smaller, separate parts (breaking down).
L-5 Synthesis	Synthesis questions are those in which you utilize the basic information in a new, original or unique way (creating).

L-6 Evaluation These are questions which help us decide on the value of our information. They enable us to make judgements about the information (predicting).

According to Bloom (1956), the major purpose for constructing the taxonomy of educational objectives was to facilitate communication. It was conceived of as a method for improving the exchange of ideas and materials among test workers, as well as other people concerned with educational research and curriculum development. A more detailed description of the levels and skills can be found in Appendix 1.

Most educators will agree that the upper four levels of the taxonomy, Application, Analysis, Synthesis and Evaluation represent the so-called higher thinking processes. Questions that contain the elements or processes of these taxonomy levels are designed to engage the learner in behavior which requires a more abstract, sophisticated integration of content and experience. There is a complexity of thinking generated at these levels which is not found at the lower levels of the taxonomy, Knowledge and Comprehension. The higher level questions require the student, a) to concentrate and observe details; b) to relate past experience with new data for the purpose of creating unique relationships, and c) to judge the validity of this new information which might be used in predicting future events.

We have often heard that process is more important than fact (or product) and that, as teachers, we must consistently facilitate process learning in our classrooms, regardless of the proliferation of materials designed for the Knowledge and Comprehension thinking levels. To provide an equalizer for the preponderance of lower level curriculum experiences, one must carefully develop material, and arrange encounters for the learner that will stimulate and support higher level thinking processes.

In addition to using children's literature for good questioning, we suggest teachers consider using these practices in all areas of instruction. Good questioning can be used effectively in the following learning experiences:

Category	Description
1. Demonstrations	In demonstrating a new skill or learning activity, the teacher may ask students questions to facilitate meaning.
2. Discussions	General discussions about current event topics offer teachers an excellent opportunity to get students to think.
3. Multi-Media Presentations	Media can create a stimulating encounter for young children. The teacher can ask the students either general type questions or questions specifically related to an event or situation viewed by the class.
4. Field Trips	The effectiveness of a particular field trip relates to the ability of the teacher to raise certain questions. These questions will enable students to integrate previous meanings with the field trip experience.

5. Debates/Role Playing	These activities have great potential for involving students in questioning. They are self-directed, student initiated and highly motivating.
6. Independent Study	The teacher can monitor a student's progress in an independent study through questioning. This provides the student and teacher with an opportunity to analyze the knowledge gained and the direction the student is taking.

Questions are the creative acts of intelligence.

Frank Kingdon

While these activities are conducive to good questioning, not all questions are planned. A teacher who practices good questioning in all aspects of the curriculum will undoubtedly use questioning in a spontaneous natural way. Once the proper climate has been established, teachers and students will engage freely and openly in spontaneous questioning. This may lead to further inquiry by the students. It is our contention that thinking skills at a qualitative level can be enhanced through effective and appropriately-timed questions and discussion sessions.

According to Dorothy Sisk (1974), teachers need to become more aware that synthesizing, summarizing, and concluding can be done quite adequately by the students. Allowing students these opportunities will increase the likelihood that they will experience learning at a higher process level. If a teacher always has the concluding statement, the student realizes that this skill is one he/she need not develop.

How Can the Taxonomy of Questions Help Teachers?

Students frequently do not develop skills in using or creating ideas because they have insufficient opportunities to practice these forms of thought.

Morris M. Sanders

The following guide has been prepared by Sisk, D. (1974), for the purpose of helping teachers pose multi-level questions:

Question Guide

Purpose	Question
To build vocabulary	Do any of you know another meaning of the word "levity" as it was used to describe this situation?
To encourage interpretive thinking	Here we have further information and data; do you have any new ideas or hypotheses?
To encourage planning	How might we go about testing this idea?
To encourage predicting	What do you think will happen when Caliban sees Miranda?
To encourage creative thinking	How might we go about solving this predicament in another fashion?

The taxonomy of questions offers teachers several interesting possibilities relating to the teaching/learning. These possibilities will be presented in random order, considering individual differences have a significant influence on the usability and success of a particular approach to questioning. The following are strategies which integrate the taxonomy with various curricular components:

STRATEGY 1:   *Selection of Instructional Material*

The taxonomy could be used as criteria for determining the appropriateness of specific content. Is the material aimed at a specific level of thinking and, if so, at what level and complexity?

STRATEGY 2:   *Building Curriculum*

As one plans differentiated learning activities for students, it might be helpful to use the various skills, e.g., verbs, related to particular thinking levels. Kaplan, S. (1974) lists numerous verbs for curriculum development. Appendix 11, Clark, B. (1979) presents an interesting model called the Taxonomy Circle, which is a good technique. Included in the circle are the taxonomy levels, suggested activities, and possible products to be developed.

STRATEGY 3:   *Building Questions From Reading Material*

In developing the questions in this text, we used both the taxonomy and verb delineations. It was helpful to have had several models and descriptions of the taxonomy while preparing the questions.

11

STRATEGY 4:   *Independent Study*

One of the major points in support of independent study is that higher level thinking skills are experienced by the learner in a natural, reality-based way. The teacher could analyze the student's activities using taxonomy as criterion.

STRATEGY 5:   *Student Selected Activities*

Providing students with decision-making opportunities is crucial to the educational process. We have seen one teacher use the taxonomy in the following manner: Students were asked to select from column one a theme, issue or problem. Next, they had to select a process from an extensive list of verbs associated with the taxonomy. Finally, they had to select a means for displaying their project, i.e., products. While this may seem highly structured, it does allow for student decision making, and it familiarizes the students with the process' terminology.

STRATEGY 6:   *Analyze Student Initiated Verbal*
Interactions

In group discussion activities, you may want to evaluate the quality and type of questions being initiated by certain students. Newton, F. (1970), has demonstrated that certain behaviors of an inquirer can be accurately observed and classified. Then we might consider using the taxonomy as a means of measuring student verbal interactions at different intervals during the school year.

12

The strategies listed above represent several possible uses for the taxonomy. We recognize that the use of these strategies will vary among different teaching styles. However, the taxonomy does provide some structure and organization to the curriculum process. If used appropriately (not in isolation) it can be advantageous to the teacher and student.

In exploring the uses of the Taxonomy of Objectives, Sanders, N. (1966), suggests three hypotheses:

1. Students who have more practice with intellectual skills will develop them to a greater degree than those who have less practice.

2. After a teacher studies the taxonomy, he/she is likely to offer students a greater variety of intellectual experiences than he/she did before.

3. A greater emphasis on the teaching of the intellectual skills (other than the memory level) will not decrease the amount of knowledge the student retains.

Three factors are presented by Sanders, N. (1966), which reflect the kind of thinking that is brought about in the minds of students by any questions: First, the nature of the questions. Second, one must be aware of the knowledge of the subject that each student brings to the classroom. The third factor that enters into the classification of a question concerns the instruction that precedes the asking of a question.

For the most part, teachers can anticipate the amount of knowledge students have on a subject and the mental process they will use to arrive at an answer.

The following points are offered by Carin, A., and Sund, R., (1978) concerning a questioning classroom environment:

1. The development of human talent and a positive self-concept hinges on the ability of the teacher to ask stimulating questions. This is basic to student-centered instruction.

2. The classification of questions assists instructors in determining how well they are teaching at the higher levels of instruction.

3. Proper questioning is a sophisticated art of teaching.

4. Higher level questions may be planned before class or spontaneously created through student interaction.

5. Fundamental to improving questioning techniques and formulating superior questions is the necessity of proper classification.

6. Research indicates that teachers specifically trained to ask better questions improve significantly in constructing and using them in the classroom. They become more adept at stimulating human potential.

7. Teachers who increase their wait-time in classroom discussions are likely to get more creative, productive thinking, longer and better responses, and a better quality of student-initiated questions. (Appendix III, *What Happens to Students When Longer Wait-Times Occur?*)

Teachers who maintain classroom environments in which students have freedom to ask questions, to theorize, and to respond to the questions raised by others will observe optimal changes in student behavior. These behavioral changes are described by the following student actions:

1. Asks a series of questions related to the one variable within the problem.

2. Sharpens a subsequent message to fine clarity after having had teacher seek clarity on previous occasions.

3. Asks to be allowed to get "his own answer."

4. Goes to data source spontaneously.

5. Follows the statement of a theory with a data probe to test it.

6. Shares a cause (theory) and doesn't ask the teacher to confirm it.

7. Shares an inference that coincides with data he/she has generated.

Some of these student actions may seem difficult to observe in any ordinary classroom. However, as one begins to concentrate on the effects of a questioning environment, one develops a proficiency at observing specific behaviors, such as the ones listed above. It is rewarding to observe these changes in student behavior, after having created an appropriate climate and practiced good questioning strategies.

THE ROLE OF THE TEACHER
IN QUESTIONING

1. It is not the intention of the writers to present these stories in any particular sequence. All questions need not be used for each story. If desired, questions from certain taxonomy levels may be omitted.

2. The language presented in the questions may be refined or adjusted to meet the needs of the individual children.

3. We encourage teachers to develop their own questions for other stories they wish to read to the class.

4. Advanced students should be encouraged to develop questions using the taxonomy levels.

5. The questions may be presented to the entire class or to small groups.

6. We encourage teachers to practice longer wait-time when initiating questions.

7. In monitoring and evaluating the types and levels of questions, we recommend the use of a tape recorder. This procedure can be used periodically to analyze discussion periods where questioning is the focus of the learning encounter.

8. Listen to discussion periods in other classrooms. Compare your questioning techniques with the techniques of other staff members.

9. Discuss the different types and levels of questions with the students. Encourage them to use the appropriate terminology and/or classification system while they are involved in discussion groups or when they are inquiring about certain data.

Why Mosquitoes Buzz In People's Ear

by Verna Aardema

The story reveals how a little mosquito affects the actions and behavior of all the animals in the jungle.

LEVEL 1 (KNOWLEDGE)

○ Who was the first animal to encounter the mosquito?

○ List all the animals affected by the mosquito's actions.

○ What animal was in charge of the council?

○ Who did not want to make the sun so that the day can come?

LEVEL 2 (COMPREHENSION)

○ Explain why the python hid from the iguana.

○ Explain why the rabbit startled the crow.

○ Explain why the crow alarmed the monkey.

○ Explain how the monkey killed the owlet.

LEVEL 3 (APPLICATION)

○ Describe how a mosquito can annoy you.

○ Describe other things that might cause a reaction and change the behavior of the animals.

○ What animals might be affected by a mosquito in your neighborhood?

○ List them in order of how they would be affected.

○ Could this happen to people. If so, how?

LEVEL 4 (ANALYSIS)

○ Describe which animal was the most careless in his action.

○ Which part in the story could the chain of events have stopped the easiest? Explain.

○ Which action by an animal was the most unrealistic? Why?

○ Which action by an animal would you consider the "most normal reaction"?

LEVEL 5 (SYNTHESIS)

○ Suppose the lion was involved. How might he have behaved in the chain of events? Whom would he have disturbed?

○ Describe a situation where a mosquito could affect the behavior of several people. Create a chain of events.

○ Change one of the animals in the story. Tell the story with a new animal.

○ Suppose the mosquito was brought to trial by the animal council. What might have happened?

LEVEL 6 (EVALUATION)

○ Predict how these animals might react if another similar situation occurs where animals are being disturbed.

○ Could a chain of events like the one described in the story really happen? If so, how?

○ Who was your favorite animal character in the story?

○ How else might a mosquito affect the behavior and actions of other animals? Or people?

Mr. Popper's Penguins

by Richard and Florence Atwater

An amusing story about a man named Mr. Popper and his twelve talented penguins, from Mr. Popper's house to theatres across America—and finally off to the North Pole.

LEVEL 1 (KNOWLEDGE)

○ Who was Mr. Popper's first and favorite penguin?

○ Where did Captain Cook sleep while at Mr. Popper's house?

○ Who gave Mr. Popper his penguin?

○ What was Mr. Popper's penguin called?

○ Name as many penguins as you can.

LEVEL 2 (COMPREHENSION)

○ Describe how Captain Cook was saved from dying.

○ Describe some of the things the Popper family did to make the penguins comfortable at home.

○ Explain what the penguins did as part of their act called Popper's Performing Penguins. Be specific.

○ Explain why Admiral Drake wanted the penguins to go to the North Pole.

LEVEL 3 (APPLICATION)

○ How would you take care of the penguins if they were yours?

○ What would you have done with the ten baby penguins if they were yours?

○ Could you have taken off from school for ten weeks in order to travel with Popper's Performing Penguins. If so, how?

○ Do you think penguins would be good pets to have? If so, why?

LEVEL 4 (ANALYSIS)

○ Which event in the story did you enjoy the most? Explain.

○ Which event in the story was the most unreal? Explain.

○ How would you describe Mr. Popper? What were his characteristics?

○ Why did the audiences seem to totally enjoy Popper's Performing Penguins? Be specific.

LEVEL 5 (SYNTHESIS)

○ If Captain Cook were your pet penguin, name several places you would like to take him to visit.

○ Instead of an ice box, how else could you have kept Captain Cook comfortable? Name some ways.

○ Suppose Mr. Popper had a dog and some cats, how would the penguins have gotten along? Would they have traveled with the Popper family?

○ Think of other funny events that could have taken place when Mr. Popper took Captain Cook to town.

LEVEL 6 (EVALUATION)

○ Why would it be difficult to keep penguins in your home? Explain.

○ Do you think penguins can be trained to perform as they did in this story? If so, why?

○ Predict what might happen if you were to have pet penguins in your neighborhood.

○ Did Mr. Popper make a right decision when he sailed to the North Pole with his penguins. Explain.

Blubber

by Judy Blume

A fat kid named Linda gets picked on by her classmates. It's cruel, it's unfair, but Linda's peers do everything to mock and tease her! When the principal found out about the situation things changed!

LEVEL 1 (KNOWLEDGE)

○ Who was called Blubber?

○ What did Linda's classmates do to her?

○ How did the principal find out about how Linda was being treated?

○ Name some things that were on the list called "How to Have Fun with Blubber"?

LEVEL 2 (COMPREHENSION)

○ Describe what Linda was like.

○ Explain what the kids did for Halloween.

○ How did Jill and Tracy get into trouble? Explain.

○ Describe what it was like in Mrs. Minish's fifth-grade class.

LEVEL 3 (APPLICATION)

○ Have you ever seen children being cruel to another child? If yes, explain.

○ How could this name calling be stopped?

○ What could Mrs. Minish do to help the situation?

○ What other things do children get picked on for in school? Name them.

LEVEL 4 (ANALYSIS)

○ Compare Jill and Linda's personalities.

○ Which event in the story made you the most angry.

○ Why do you think Jill liked to tease Linda about being fat?

○ How would you describe Linda's feelings after being teased by her classmates?

LEVEL 5 (SYNTHESIS)

○ Suppose Jill was obese. How would she have handled being called "Blubber"?

○ Think of some ways Linda could have stopped the children from picking on her.

○ Describe what Linda's mother and father were like.

○ Suppose Mrs. Minish was obese. How might that have changed the story?

LEVEL 6 (EVALUATION)

○ Judge the character of children who pick on other children.

○ Predict other difficult situations for Linda in the future.

○ Which event in the story did you find to be most unpleasant? Why?

○ Predict how many children in America are being called "Blubber" or similar kinds of things.

Freckle Juice

by Judy Blume

Andrew finds Nicky Lane's freckles fascinating! He even purchases "Freckle Juice" from Sharon for fifty cents!

LEVEL 1 (KNOWLEDGE)

o Who had freckles in Miss Kelly's class?

o Who gave Andrew the "Freckles Juice"?

o How did Andrew finally make freckles?

o What did Miss Kelly give Andrew?

LEVEL 2 (COMPREHENSION)

o Explain how Andrew got "Freckle Juice."

o Describe the contents of the "Freckle Juice."

o Describe Andrew's reaction to the "Freckle Juice."

o Tell what Andrew had to do to remove his fake freckles.

LEVEL 3 (APPLICATION)

o Who do you know who has freckles?

o Did you ever want to look like someone else? How? Why? When?

o Can freckles be removed from someone's face? If yes, how?

o How does someone get freckles?

25

LEVEL 4 (ANALYSIS)

○ Analyze Nicky Lane's feelings about why Andrew wanted freckles so badly.

○ Why did Sharon make "Freckle Juice"?

○ Why did Andrew make fake freckles?

○ Analyze how Miss Kelly dealt with Andrew's fake freckles.

LEVEL 5 (SYNTHESIS)

○ Think of other imaginative ways of removing someone's freckles.

○ Make up your own formula for "Freckle Juice."

○ Suppose the "Freckle Juice" worked giving Andrew all the freckles he wanted. What might happen with Sharon's formula?

○ List reasons why someone might want to have freckles.

LEVEL 6 (EVALUATION)

○ Judge why Andrew wanted freckles.

○ Predict what might happen if Sharon's "Freckle Juice" really worked.

○ Why is it wrong to wish for certain human qualities?

○ If the "Freckle Juice" worked, would there be many children wanting freckles? Explain.

Otherwise Known As Sheila The Great

by Judy Blume

It seemed as if there were two Sheilas—both ten years old—Sheila The Great and Sheila Tubman. And a summer in the strange suburban world of Tarrytown, complete with such terrors as swimming lessons, thunderstorms, and a resident beagle might just undermine "The Great" image once and for all.

LEVEL 1 (KNOWLEDGE)

○ What was Sheila's sister's name?

○ Where did the story take place?

○ Who was Sheila's best friend during her summer vacation at Tarrytown?

○ What did Sheila have to protect in the room where she slept?

LEVEL 2 (COMPREHENSION)

○ Describe Sheila's reaction to Jennifer.

○ Describe how Sheila published her first and last camp newsletter.

○ Explain what happened during a hide-and-seek game at Mouse's house.

○ Describe Sheila's attitude and feelings about swimming.

LEVEL 3 (APPLICATION)

○ How does Tarrytown compare to places you have spent the summer at? Be specific.

o How does Sheila's summer camp compare to a summer camp you attended?

o Whom does Sheila remind you of in your neighborhood?

o What would you have done to protect the models in Sheila's room?

LEVEL 4 (ANALYSIS)

o Compare Sheila with Libby. How were they the same? How were they different?

o Analyze Sheila's attitude about herself. What did she think of herself and what she could do?

o Analyze Sheila's negative reaction to swimming lessons.

o Why did Sheila like Mouse so much?

LEVEL 5 (SYNTHESIS)

o Suppose the story took place in the winter. How would it have been different?

o Think of other things Sheila and Mouse could have done during the summer.

o Suppose Libby was an older brother. How would this have affected Sheila? Be specific.

o Suppose Sheila just moved next door to you. How would you deal with her in your first meeting.

LEVEL 6 (EVALUATION)

o Judge whether Sheila would be a good "best friend."

○ Which event in the story did you most enjoy? Why?

○ How would Sheila have gotten along with Bobby Egran, Professor Egran's son?

○ What made Sheila feel she was "Sheila the Great?" Explain.

Superfudge

by Judy Blume

Nothing is simple for twelve-year-old Peter Hatcher. And nothing drives him up the wall quicker than the off-the-wall antics of his little brother, Farley Drexel Hatcher—otherwise known as Fudge.

LEVEL 1 (KNOWLEDGE)

○ What was Peter's new baby sister's name?

○ Where did Peter's family move to?

○ Who became Peter's best friend in Princeton?

○ What did Peter and Alex do to make money?

LEVEL 2 (COMPREHENSION)

○ Explain why the Hatcher's moved to Princeton.

○ Explain why Fudge was moved to a new kindergarten?

○ Describe what Princeton was like.

○ Tell why Fudge's bird was so interesting.

LEVEL 3 (APPLICATION)

○ How would you feel about moving to another state?

○ How would you feel if your family announced that there would be a new baby coming soon?

○ Do you have a brother or sister like Fudge? If so, how is she or he like Fudge?

○ How would you make friends if you were to move to another state?

LEVEL 4 (ANALYSIS)

○ Compare Fudge to your little brother or sister.

○ Analyze Peter's attitude about moving from New York City.

○ Which character in the story did you find most interesting? Why?

○ Describe an ever in the story where Fudge embarrassed his family.

LEVEL 5 (SYNTHESIS)

○ "Fudge goes to Princeton." Make-up some new situations where Fudge gets in trouble.

○ Think of some other things Fudge and Alex could sell in their neighborhood.

○ Create a new character whom the boys meet in Princeton.

○ Suppose the move to Princeton was permanent, think of ways Peter could get back to New York City and see his friends.

LEVEL 6 (EVALUATION)

○ Judge whether Peter is a good older brother to Fudge.

○ Predict Fudge's behavior toward baby Tooties as she gets older.

○ Indicate your favorite event in the story and tell why you have selected that one.

○ What kinds of difficulties might Fudge experience as he grows older? Explain.

Tales Of A Fourth Grade Nothing

by Judy Blume

The story is about a fourth grader named Peter Hatcher who had to endure the mischievous behavior of his little brother "Fudge." The author provides numerous accounts of "Fudge's" never ending, pestering actions which seem to make living with him... impossible!

LEVEL 1 (KNOWLEDGE)

○ Identify three situations where Fudge annoyed his brother Peter.

○ Recall what Fudge did to his brother Peter's transportation project.

○ Tell how Fudge got the name "Fang."

○ Tell what happened to Dribble.

LEVEL 2 (COMPREHENSION)

○ How did Mr. Hatcher get Fudge to eat?

○ Retell how Fudge annoyed Mr. Hatcher's client, Mr. Yarby.

○ Why did Mrs. Hatcher leave Fudge at home with a babysitter?

○ Explain how they got Dribble out of Fudge's stomach.

LEVEL 3 (APPLICATION)

○ If you were Peter how would you deal with Fudge's behavior?

○ Tell how your mother would have limited Fudge's disruptive behavior.

○ If Fudge was the brother of your best friend, what advice would you give him about how to get along with someone like Fudge?

○ Is it possible to keep Fudge from causing so many problems? If so, how?

LEVEL 4 (ANALYSIS)

○ What three words would you use to describe Fudge?

○ Which of Peter's problems (caused by Fudge) was the most difficult to deal with?

○ Compare Peter's problems with Fudge to other problems a fourth grader might encounter.

○ What part of the story did you believe was the most serious? Why?

LEVEL 5 (SYNTHESIS)

○ Suppose Fudge was a girl. Would this have changed the story?

○ Retell the story. Make up two more problem situations involving Fudge.

○ Invent three different ways to keep Fudge out of Peter's room.

○ Imagine what would have happened had Peter and Fudge had two or three brothers and/or sisters.

LEVEL 6 (EVALUATION)

○ Describe how Peter felt when his pet turtle "Dribbles" was eaten.

○ Judge how effective the Hatchers were in handling Fudge.

○ Choose the person with whom you would have more in common: Peter or Fudge.

○ Predict how Peter and Fudge will get along in the future.

The Computer Nut

by Betsy Byars

An amusing story of a young girl who makes contact with an alien through her personal computer. Getting others to believe her is the challenge!

LEVEL 1 (KNOWLEDGE)

○ What was the first think Katie created on her computer?

○ Where was Katie's computer located?

○ What did BB—9 want to do most on his visit to earth?

○ Who was with Katie when personal contact was made with BB-9?

LEVEL 2 (COMPREHENSION)

○ Explain how Katie was contacted by BB-9.

○ Describe how Katie and Linda went about trying to find out the identify of BB-9.

○ Explain why BB-9 wanted to visit planet Earth.

○ Describe BB-9's encounter at the football stadium.

LEVEL 3 (APPLICATION)

○ How is this story like E.T.? Compare.

○ Why is it possible to communicate with others through the use of a computer? Explain.

○ What types of businesses use computers to communicate? Explain.

o Compare the telephone with the computer. How are they alike?

LEVEL 4 (ANALYSIS)

o Why is this story fiction?

o Analyze the reactions of the characters in the story regarding the initial belief of BB-9.

o Analyze the relationship and interactions of Katie and her family.

o Compare Katie's reaction to the first encounter with BB-9 to how you would have reacted.

LEVEL 5 (SYNTHESIS)

o Instead of an alien who else could have contacted Katie through a computer.

o Make a list of other reasons why BB-9 wanted to visit each person.

o Suppose BB—9 was a boy from another country. How would the story have been different?

o Make up a new ending to the story by having BB—9 stay with Katie and her family.

LEVEL 6 (EVALUATION)

o Make a list of reasons why this story is fiction?

o Decide whether boys and girls will be able to communicate through the use of computers in the future. If yes, explain.

o Evaluate the quality of BB-9's jokes.

o If we are ever contacted by aliens, which telecommunication system would be the one most likely to be used?

The 18th Emergency

by Betsy Byars

Ezzie tells Benjie about 17 emergency situations and how to deal with them—however, the 18th emergency has Benjie, a fifth grader, meeting up with the class bully, an angry, powerful boy named Marv Hammerman.

LEVEL 1 (KNOWLEDGE)

○ Who was Benjie's best friend?

○ Name several of Ezzie's emergencies and how to survive each?

○ Who was Mr. Casino?

○ Who did Benjie want to avoid in the story?

LEVEL 2 (COMPREHENSION)

○ Explain how Benjie and Ezzie helped Mr. Casino.

○ Describe Benjie's fifth-grade class.

○ Describe what Marv Hammerman was like.

○ Describe the confrontation between Benjie and Hammerman at the end of the story.

LEVEL 3 (APPLICATION)

○ What types of emergencies have you dreamed about?

○ Do you have a friend like Ezzie? If yes, describe this person.

○ Have you ever been in a situation where someone wanted to fight you? Explain.

o What would you have done to avoid Hammerman if you were Benjie?

LEVEL 4 (ANALYSIS)

o Which emergency was the most terrifying? Explain.

o Compare Marv Hammerman to someone you know who has similar bully traits.

o Analyze Benjie's personality.

o Compare your emergency dreams with the emergency dreams mentioned in the story.

LEVEL 5 (SYNTHESIS)

o Make up five new emergency situations, including creative ways of surviving.

o Think of three things you would want to say to Marv Hammerman if you had an opportunity to meet him.

o How else could Benjie have handled the Hammerman situation? Be specific.

o If you were attacked by a crocodile how might you survive? Be creative.

LEVEL 6 (EVALUATION)

o Judge which emergency could really happen if you weren't careful.

o Predict how Benjie and Hammerman will get along in the future.

o Are most children faced with an ''18th Emergency'' like the one in the story? Explain.

o Evaluate Benjie and Ezzie's relationship.

The Pinballs

by Betsy Byars

Three young people are put into a foster home. Together they share the loneliness and uncertainty of tomorrow. They are just like Pinballs being knocked around. However, at the end they realize that they don't have to be Pinballs—that they can do something with their lives.

LEVEL 1 (KNOWLEDGE)

o Who were the three foster children?

o Name the foster parents.

o What happened to Harvey's legs.

o Who had taken care of Thomas J most of his life?

o What gift really pleased Harvey while he was in the hospital?

LEVEL 2 (COMPREHENSION)

o Describe Thomas J's life prior to coming to live with the Mason's.

o Describe Carlie's life prior to coming to live with the Mason's.

o Explain how Harvey's father ran him over and broke his legs.

o Tell why Mrs. Mason was such a good foster mother.

LEVEL 3 (APPLICATION)

o Do you know anyone that lives in a foster home? Explain.

o How would you feel if you were told that you must live in a foster home?

o Which child had the most difficult life prior to moving in with Mrs. Mason?

o Who helps foster children in your community or country?

LEVEL 4 (ANALYSIS)

o Compare Thomas J with Harvey. How were they different?

o Which event in the story made you realize how difficult it is being a foster child?

o Why would Mr. & Mrs. Mason want to take in three children?

o Why was the comparison made between Pinballs and foster children? Explain.

LEVEL 5 (SYNTHESIS)

o Tell what will happen as the three children grow up. What kinds of jobs will they find.

o Invent a fourth child for the Masons. Describe this new child.

o If you wanted to do something kind and thoughtful for the three children, what would you do?

o Make up nicknames for Harvey, Carlie, and Thomas J.

LEVEL 6 (EVALUATION)

o Judge whether or not this could happen to these children—being separated from their families.

o What would be the most difficult responsibility for the Masons in taking care of the foster children?

○ Predict what the relationship will be between the three children and the Masons in the future.

○ How many foster children are there currently in the United States?

The TV Kid

by Betsy Byars

Lennie is fascinated by TV. If he isn't watching it, he is imagining himself appearing on different shows. When Lennie is bitten by a snake, he uses his TV images to ease the pain. An interesting adventure of a young boy with a marvelous imagination.

LEVEL 1 (KNOWLEDGE)

○ Where did Lennie live?

○ On which TV show did Lennie want to appear on?

○ What happened to Lennie while he was at the old stone house?

○ Who rescued Lennie and took him to the hospital?

LEVEL 2 (COMPREHENSION)

○ Describe where Lennie lived.

○ Describe the kinds of chores Lennie did for his mom at the Fairy Land Motel.

○ Explain Lennie's fascination with TV. What did he really like about TV?

○ Tell how Lennie was bitten by the snake.

LEVEL 3 (APPLICATION)

○ What TV show would you like to appear on? Explain.

○ What TV shows do you "visualize in your mind"? Explain.

○ What would be your feelings if you have been hiding under the porch while the policeman searched?

o Are lots of kids fascinated by TV? How? Explain.

LEVEL 4 (ANALYSIS)

o Which event in the story describes Lennie's addiction to TV?

o Should Lennie have stayed under the porch when the policeman first appeared?

o Compare Lennie's imagination to yours.

o Which TV show mentioned by Lennie would be your favorite?

LEVEL 5 (SYNTHESIS)

o Suppose Lennie was invited to appear on a famous TV Game Show. How would he react?

o What would it be like to be Lennie's brother or sister?

o Suppose the policeman didn't find Lennie. What would have happened?

o If Lennie were to write a book for children entitled "The Wonderful World of TV," what kinds of things would he say to the children?

LEVEL 6 (EVALUATION)

o Judge whether Lennie should have hidden from the policeman.

o What are the advantages of TV?

o What are the disadvantages of TV?

o Predict how Lennie will use his imagination in the future.

Ramona The Brave

by Beverly Cleary

Ramona the Brave is about a spunky little six-year old who "says what she thinks," "acts impulsively," and makes her own decisions about school and about life.

LEVEL 1 (KNOWLEDGE)

○ What was Ramona's sister's name?

○ What did Ramona do in school that annoyed Mrs. Griggs?

○ What was the "bad word" Ramona used in the story?

○ Name the event in the story which helped Ramona feel better about herself.

LEVEL 2 (COMPREHENSION)

○ Describe what Ramona did to Susan's drawing.

○ Describe what Mrs. Griggs said in Ramona's report card.

○ Explain Ramona's reaction to her new room.

○ Explain why Ramona came to school with one shoe missing.

LEVEL 3 (APPLICATION)

○ If Ramona were your sister, what things would you want to say to her?

○ Who do you know that is like Ramona? Describe them.

○ How could Mrs. Griggs have made Ramona feel better about herself?

o What would you do if someone copied your drawing? Explain.

LEVEL 4 (ANALYSIS)

o Compare Ramona to her sister, Beezus. How were they alike? How were they not alike?

o Why did Ramona want to switch from Mrs. Griggs' class?

o Analyze how Ramona's classmates acted toward her. Be specific.

o Why did Ramona seem to like Mr. Cardoza?

LEVEL 5 (SYNTHESIS)

o Instead of an older sister, suppose Ramona had a younger sister. How might that have influenced her behavior?

o Create three other conflicts between Ramona and her classmates.

o Describe the kinds of situations in which Ramona will get involved in Grades 3 and 4.

o Change the story so that Ramona and her teacher are extremely close and supportive of each other.

LEVEL 6 (EVALUATION)

o How was this story real? Explain.

o Judge whether you would like to be Ramona's friend.

o Judge whether Ramona made a good decision when she threw her shoe at the dog.

o Tell why you would like to be Ramona's classmate and friend.

Hornswoggle Magic

by Otto Coontz

When Casey and Milton first meet Jenny Sphinx, they think she's the strangest woman they've ever seen. Jenny turns out to be a boon. She's got a magical solution to Mr. Wiseman's problem, and Casey and Milton have a wonderful zany time helping her out.

LEVEL 1 (KNOWLEDGE)

○ What did Milton's father own?

○ Who did Casey meet in the subway?

○ What made the automat malfunction?

○ Who asked Mr. Wiseman to return to his newsstand?

LEVEL 2 (COMPREHENSION)

○ Describe what Jenny Sphinx looked like.

○ Describe how Casey and Milton got into the subway late at night.

○ Explain what the hornswoggle coin did to the automat.

○ Tell what happened to the subway ticket machine.

LEVEL 3 (APPLICATION)

○ Do you know anyone who lost a job because of technology?

○ If you were Casey, how would you have helped Mr. Wiseman?

○ Would you have gone down into the subway at night with a friend? Explain.

○ Have you ever seen an old person with bags? Explain.

LEVEL 4 (ANALYSIS)

○ Name the event in the story which makes it a fantasy.

○ Analyze Jenny Sphinx. What type of person was she? Explain.

○ Compare what Casey and Milton did to something daring you and your friends have done?

○ Why do you think Casey wanted to help Mr. Wiseman as much as she did?

LEVEL 5 (SYNTHESIS)

○ What other types of magic can the hornswoggle coins produce?

○ Describe what it would be like living in the subway.

○ Retell the story with Casey and Milton using glue on the automat machines.

○ Tell about another stranger Casey and Milton might meet one night in the subway.

LEVEL 6 (EVALUATION)

○ Judge whether Jenny Sphinx was a good person.

○ Evaluate the choice of using glue on the automat machines.

○ List five qualities that Casey had.

○ Predict what will happen to Mr. Wiseman's newsstand in the future.

Charlie And The Chocolate Factory

by Roald Dahl

The story is about a boy named Charlie who loved chocolate. His fantasy was realized when he won a special trip to the amazing Chocolate Factory. Along with four other winners, Charlie experienced all the wonders of Mr. Wonka's famous Chocolate Factory.

LEVEL 1 (KNOWLEDGE)

○ With whom did Charlie live?

○ How did Charlie get to visit the Chocolate Factory?

○ Who were the five people who won the Golden Tickets?

○ What happened at the conclusion of Charlie's visit through the Chocolate Factory?

LEVEL 2 (COMPREHENSION)

○ Describe how Charlie and his family lived.

○ Describe what Mr. Wonka looked like.

○ Explain the different rooms in Mr. Wonka's Chocolate Factory.

○ Describe what happens to the four people who along with Charlie tour the Chocolate Factory.

LEVEL 3 (APPLICATION)

○ How would you have behaved if you had gone on the tour of the Chocolate Factory?

○ How else could Mr. Wonka have selected people for his tour?

○ Tell how you would have conducted a tour of the Chocolate Factory.

○ Who would you bring with you on a tour through the Chocolate Factory?

LEVEL 4 (ANALYSIS)

○ Which of the five Golden Tickets winners most resembles you? Why?

○ Which room in the Chocolate Factory you like to visit the most? Why?

○ What events in the story points out the craziness of Mr. Wonka?

○ In what ways is the Chocolate Factory similar or dissimilar to Disney World? Be specific.

LEVEL 5 (SYNTHESIS)

○ Predict what might have happened had one hundred people gone on the tour through the Chocolate Factory.

○ Think of other types of special rooms Mr. Wonka could have in his Chocolate Factory.

○ What else could have happened to the people touring the Chocolate Factory?

○ Describe how Charlie will run the Chocolate Factory in the future.

LEVEL 6 (EVALUATION)

○ Judge whether Mr. Wonka was a good owner of a Chocolate Factory.

○ Choose the person with whom you would most like to be friends with: Violet Beauregarde, Augustus Gloop, Mike Teavee, or Veruca Salt. Why?

○ Evaluate Mr. Wonka's plan for selecting a person to give the Chocolate Factory to.

○ Tell why you would be a good owner of a Chocolate Factory.

George's Marvelous Medicine

by Roald Dahl

"Open your mouth wide, Grandma," George said. The old hag opened her small wrinkled mouth, showing disgusting pale brown teeth. "Here we go!" and her whole body shot up whoosh into the air. Up she went like a jack in the box—-and she didn't come down.

LEVEL 1 (KNOWLEDGE)

○ What was George's marvelous plan?

○ What happened to Grandma after she took George's medicine?

○ Who else had George's medicine?

○ What finally happened to Grandma?

LEVEL 2 (COMPREHENSION)

○ Describe the contents of George's marvelous medicine.

○ Explain what happened to the animals after taking the medicine.

○ Describe what happened with the other medicine George made.

○ Tell what happened to Grandma after she took the new medicine.

LEVEL 3 (APPLICATION)

○ Do you know anyone who is like George's Grandma?

○ Have you ever taken medicine which made your mouth and throat burn? Describe.

○ Why are most Grandmas very sweet and nice people?

51

○ Have you ever gotten angry when asked—"to do this"—"to do that"—"to do this"—"to do that"? Explain.

LEVEL 4 (ANALYSIS)

○ Why did George want to give his Grandma a new type of medicine?

○ Which event in the story was the "most strange"?

○ Compare George's Grandma to your Grandma.

○ Tell why George's medicine is fantasy—unreal.

LEVEL 5 (SYNTHESIS)

○ To whom would you want to give George's medicine?

○ Do you think George will ever try his own medicine?

○ Make up some names for George's medicine.

○ How else could George have made money with his magical medicine? Explain.

LEVEL 6 (EVALUATION)

○ Judge what type of person Grandma was.

○ How are real medicines made?

○ Did Grandma like her new body? Explain.

○ What kinds of problems would George have if he really did invent a "Magical Medicine"?

James And The Giant Peach

by Roald Dahl

James is given a gift of magic. Magic takes hold of an old peach tree. And all of a sudden a giant peach appears with living creatures inside. James explores/meets new friends and travels across the ocean to America. "An amazing, delightful adventure that invigorates the imagination."

LEVEL 1 (KNOWLEDGE)

○ What happened to James' parents?

○ What were James' aunts' names?

○ Who gave the magical "little green things" to James?

○ Name the insects James found inside the peach.

○ Where did their journey end?

LEVEL 2 (COMPREHENSION)

○ Describe James' journey into the peach.

○ Describe the creatures James discovered inside the peach.

○ Tell about the experiences James and his insect friends experienced while traveling to America.

○ How did James get the peach up into the air? Explain.

LEVEL 3 (APPLICATION)

○ What types of insects might you find inside a real peach?

o What will you think about the next time you eat a peach?

o What was your most vivid image in the story?

o Have you ever looked inside a peach pit? What does it look like?

LEVEL 4 (ANALYSIS)

o Who was your favorite creature in the story? Tell why.

o Which event in the story was the most thrilling?

o Which creature would make the best pet?

o Which creature would you most likely find inside a piece of fruit?

LEVEL 5 (SYNTHESIS)

o How would the story be different if it were a banana?

o Think of two additional creatures who could have lived inside the peach.

o Suppose James' aunts were waiting in New York. What might have happened?

o Suppose you had some magical "little green things," what would you do with them?

LEVEL 6 (EVALUATION)

o Decide whether you would like to have been James in this story. Explain.

o Predict what the aunts will do when they find out where James is.

○ Why does this story evoke vivid images (pictures) in your mind?

○ Tell how you might create a story like this one, only using another piece of fruit. Explain.

The Blue-Nosed Witch

by Margaret Embry

A delightful story of a young girl who is an actual "witch."
She visits with the children on Halloween and amazes them with
her powers!

LEVEL 1 (KNOWLEDGE)

○ What two things did Blanche have with her when she visited
the children?

○ Who gave Blanche and the children rotten apples?

○ What was the name of the witches' group Blanche belonged to?

○ What did Blanche bring back and give to the other witches?

LEVEL 2 (COMPREHENSION)

○ Describe Scurry No. 13

○ Describe Blanche's visit with the children on Halloween
evening.

○ Tell what Blanche did to Mr. Skinner.

○ Describe the children's costumes.

LEVEL 3 (APPLICATION)

○ Have you ever heard witch stories? Explain.

○ What do children look like when dressed as witches? Describe.

○ Whose house do you stay away from on Halloween? Explain.

○ Describe your favorite Halloween costume.

LEVEL 4 (ANALYSIS)

○ Why did the children think Blanche was one of them?

○ Why were the children scared of Mr. Skinner?

○ Compare Blanche to a witch's costume you have seen?

○ How was Blanche able to fly?

LEVEL 5 (SYNTHESIS)

○ Name other magical things Blanche could do.

○ Suppose Mr. Skinner caught Blanche. What might have happened?

○ Would you want Blanche to go trick-or-treating with you next Halloween?

○ If you lived with Blanche and the other witches, what kinds of things would you want them to do?

LEVEL 6 (EVALUATION)

○ Why was Blanche a nice witch?

○ Judge whether there are real witches.

○ Besides Blanche, who else had a good costume on Halloween evening.

○ Predict what Blanche and the children will do next Halloween.

The Hundred Dresses

by Eleanor Estes

Wanda would tell the children she had a hundred dresses at home—all lined up in her closet. They laughed and Wanda's lips would tighten as she walked off. Wanda did have the hundred dresses, and this is the story of how Peggy and Maddie came to understand about them and about what their game had meant to Wanda.

LEVEL 1 (KNOWLEDGE)

o Who picked on Wanda in the story?

o What dress did Wanda wear to school each day?

o What did Wanda and her father do?

o How did Wanda find out about the change in Peggy and Maddie's attitude?

LEVEL 2 (COMPREHENSION)

o Explain how Wanda reacted when Peggy and Maddie teased her.

o Explain how Peggy and Maddie found out that Wanda did have a hundred dresses.

o Describe what Wanda said in her letter to the class.

o Tell what Peggy and Maddie wrote in their letter to Wanda.

LEVEL 3 (APPLICATION)

o Have you ever known someone that was picked on like Wanda was in the story? Explain.

o How would you have behaved if you were one of Wanda's classmates?

o What lesson does this story teach you? Explain.

o If Wanda was your sister, how would your parents have reacted to the situation?

LEVEL 4 (ANALYSIS)

o Why did Peggy and Maddie tease Wanda? Explain.

o Describe the event in the story which made you feel empathy for Wanda.

o Why do some children get picked on more than others?

o How would you describe a person that always picks on others? Be specific.

LEVEL 5 (SYNTHESIS)

o Suppose Wanda did not have a hundred dresses, how would that have changed things?

o Suppose Wanda's father was a mean and nasty individual— what might have happened?

o If Wanda were to return home from the city, how would Peggy and Maddie treat her? Explain.

o Develop a new ending to the story. Describe it.

LEVEL 6 (EVALUATION)

o Judge why people tease and pick on others.

o Judge whether Peggy and Maddie will tease and mock others in the future. Explain.

○ Which event in the story made you very sad? Explain.

○ Which "kids" are picked on the most in schools today? Explain.

JD

by Mari Evans

In these four stories, JD finds a mysterious box which may contain a million dollars! He gets in a fight with a big kid who's beating up on a little brother. In the third story he tries very hard not to wake up one morning for school, and finally in the fourth story he sees older people shooting drugs.

LEVEL 1 (KNOWLEDGE)

○ Where did JD live?

○ Who lived with JD?

○ Why did JD not want to go to school?

○ What was the man's name who was shooting drugs in the fourth story?

LEVEL 2 (COMPREHENSION)

○ Describe how JD tried to open the mysterious little box.

○ Explain how JD survived the fight with a bigger boy.

○ Describe what would happen if JD could not pay the book rental fee in school.

○ Describe JD's encounter with the man doing drugs.

LEVEL 3 (APPLICATION)

○ Why did JD have trouble paying the book rental fee?

○ Do you get into fights in your neighborhood? Explain.

o Why is it difficult for a young boy to live with just one parent?

o How would you feel about living in a neighborhood where people used drugs? Explain.

LEVEL 4 (ANALYSIS)

o Compare JD's experiences with yours.

o Why is life difficult where JD lived?

o Analyze JD's attitude about life.

o Identify an event in the story that has happened to you.

LEVEL 5 (SYNTHESIS)

o Why would JD make a good friend if he moved to your neighborhood?

o Describe other events JD might experience living at Salem Court.

o Suppose JD's mother gets married again. How will this affect him?

o Describe what you would say to JD if you had an opportunity to play with him.

LEVEL 6 (EVALUATION)

o Judge why JD may encounter other difficult situations growing up in his neighborhood.

o Predict what kind of person JD will be when he grows up.

o Are there other kids like JD? Explain.

o Are there other housing projects like Meadow Hill.

McBroom Tells The Truth

by Sid Fleischman

There's been a lot of tomfool nonsense told about McBroom's wonderful one-acre farm—about how it was eighty acres when he bought it, and it shrank to one; and how everything grew so fast it would knock you over if you weren't careful.

LEVEL 1 (KNOWLEDGE)

o How many children did McBroom and his wife have?

o Name McBroom's children.

o Who sold McBroom his farm?

o What did the McBroom family grow on their farm?

LEVEL 2 (COMPREHENSION)

o Explain how McBroom got his land.

o Why did the crops grow so well on McBroom's land? Explain.

o How did Heck Jones try to get back his farm? Explain.

o Explain what happened to Heck Jones at the end of the story.

LEVEL 3 (APPLICATION)

o What parts of this story could be true? Explain.

o Would you have liked to have been one of McBroom's eleven red-headed youngsters? Why?

o Are there people like Heck Jones today? Explain.

○ How would your parents have kept Heck Jones away from their land? Explain.

LEVEL 4 (ANALYSIS)

○ Do you know anyone who is like McBroom?

○ Are there places where land is very fertile? Describe them.

○ How would you describe Heck Jones? Be specific.

○ How would life be different for you if you were a McBroom kid?

LEVEL 5 (SYNTHESIS)

○ Suppose McBroom was unable to grow anything on his land, what might he have done?

○ Think of other things McBroom could have grown on his land giving him huge profits.

○ Make up other stories McBroom could tell about his famous one acre farm.

○ If you were a TV talk show host, what questions would you want to ask McBroom?

LEVEL 6 (EVALUATION)

○ Predict what might have happened if the McBroom's were unable to grow anything on their land.

○ Which events in the story were totally unreal?

○ Could parents have eleven red-headed children? Why? Why not?

○ Judge what type of person McBroom was.

Chitty Chitty Bang Bang, The Magical Car

by Ian Fleming

An exciting adventure about a family and their many experiences with a magical car.

LEVEL 1 (KNOWLEDGE)

○ Where did Commander Pott get his magical car?

○ How did the car get its magical name "Chitty Chitty Bang Bang"?

○ Who kidnapped Commander Potts's two children Jeremy and Jemina?

○ How fast did the Chitty Chitty Bang Bang car go?

LEVEL 2 (COMPREHENSION)

○ Describe what the magical car looked like.

○ Explain why the car was magical.

○ Where did Commander Pott take his family?

○ How were Jeremy and Jemina found?

LEVEL 3 (APPLICATION)

○ Describe what it would be like to own a magical car.

○ Where would you want to go if you had a magical car?

○ How would your parents react if they owned Chitty Chitty Bang Bang?

○ Do you think they will ever have cars like Chitty Chitty Bang Bang? If so, explain.

LEVEL 4 (ANALYSIS)

○ Describe the most exciting event in the story. Be specific.

○ Compare Chitty Chitty Bang Bang's performance in the air and on water.

○ Compare Chitty Chitty Bang Bang with a present day car.

○ Make a list of the events in the story that indicate it is a fairy tale.

LEVEL 5 (SYNTHESIS)

○ Make Chitty Chitty Bang Bang more magical. Think of other things it might be able to do.

○ Make a list of new names for this magical car.

○ Predict what would happen if everyone had such a car.

○ Create a new ending for the story.

LEVEL 6 (EVALUATION)

○ Describe Commander Pott. What was he like? Whom does he remind you of?

○ Discuss whether you think there will ever be cars that can fly.

○ Why would you like to be like Commander Pott? Explain.

○ Which is more probably in the future: Cars that fly or cars that sail in water? Explain.

Mustard

by Charlotte Graeber

Eight-year-old Alex thinks Mustard is the most wonderful cat in the world, a cat with dignity and humor and the loudest, best purr ever. Mustard is old, but Alex stubbornly refuses to accept it. Mustard seems just fine. However, with the help of his family, Alex must come to terms with Mustard's increasing infirmities and eventual death.

LEVEL 1 (KNOWLEDGE)

○ Who was Alex's little sister?

○ What was the doctor's name?

○ Who was Barney?

○ Where did Alex's dad bury Mustard?

LEVEL 2 (COMPREHENSION)

○ Explain why everyone kept telling Alex that Mustard was old.

○ Describe what Dr. Griffith prescribed for Mustard in the beginning of the story.

○ Describe what happened to Mustard while chasing Barney.

○ How did Alex react when told of Mustard's death? Explain.

LEVEL 3 (APPLICATION)

○ How is Mustard like one of your pets? Explain.

○ How would you have taken care of Mustard had he been your pet cat? Describe.

o Why is a cat a good family pet? Explain.

o What should Alex do now that Mustard is dead?

LEVEL 4 (ANALYSIS)

o Compare Mustard to a cat that you know.

o Could the family have kept Mustard from having a heart attack? How? Explain.

o Why did Alex's family keep telling and reminding him that Mustard was an old cat?

o Compare Alex's love for Mustard to your love for your pet.

LEVEL 5 (SYNTHESIS)

o What else could have happened to Mustard as an aging cat? Explain.

o Suppose Mustard was a dog, how might the story be different? Explain.

o Tell about Mustard when he was a young cat.

o Change the ending of the story. Make it different.

LEVEL 6 (EVALUATION)

o Should Alex's family have taken care of Mustard differently? Explain.

o How do you know that Dr. Griffith was a good animal doctor? Explain.

o Predict what might have happened to Mustard if he didn't have a heart attack.

o Judge whether Mustard should be buried in the back yard.

Max And Me
And The Time Machine

by Gery Greer and Bob Ruddick

It took Steve a few moments to get his bearings. Then he realized that the time machine had worked. He was in thirteenth-century England, just where he wanted to be, but not as Steve Brandon. He's been transported into the body of Sir Robert Marshall. Later he learned that his friend Max had become Sir Robert's horse!

LEVEL 1 (KNOWLEDGE)

○ Where did the boys find the time machine?

○ Who did Steve become when placed back into thirteenth-century England?

○ What was the name of the villain in the story?

○ Who did Max become when placed back into thirteenth-century England?

LEVEL 2 (COMPREHENSION)

○ Explain how Steve (Sir Robert) became a hero.

○ Describe other ways Sir Robert became the people's favorite.

○ Describe Sir Bevis' plan to get rid of Sir Robert.

○ Explain how Sir Bevis was defeated and sent away.

LEVEL 3 (APPLICATION)

○ What ways could a time machine be helpful to society?

69

- If you were going back into history, what communication technology would you want to bring with you?

- List several different periods in history you would like to visit.

- Think of a specific period in history each person in your family would want to visit.

LEVEL 4 (ANALYSIS)

- Analyze the lifestyle of the people who lived in the castle.

- Compare Sir Bevis to a present-day TV/movie villain.

- Which event in the story was the most thrilling? Why?

- Explain why Dr. Gathergoods would have difficulty in today's medicine.

LEVEL 5 (SYNTHESIS)

- Suppose the time machine broke and could not return Steve and Max. How would they have survived? Explain.

- Describe other ways Sir Robert could have defeated Sir Bevis in competition.

- Which event in the story would you like to change? How?

- If you had a time machine, where would you want to visit? Explain.

LEVEL 6 (EVALUATION)

- What do you think Professor Flybender was like?

- Judge the relationship between Steve and Max. Be specific.

○ If your parents had a time machine, where do you think they would want to visit?

○ If everyone had a time machine, what period in history would attract many, many people?

Alexander the Great

by John Gunther

An amazing story about the dreams, ambitions, accomplishments and legends of Alexander the Great—the famous warrior and king of Macedonia. The book tells of how this young man conquered the world.

LEVEL 1 (KNOWLEDGE)

○ What was Alexander's first gift from King Phillip?

○ Who was Alexander's great and famous teacher?

○ Name some of the cities and territories Alexander conquered.

○ What were some of the things Alexander did that were cruel and unnecessary?

LEVEL 2 (COMPREHENSION)

○ Explain how Alexander's army attacked its enemy.

○ Describe how Alexander demonstrated his power and courage.

○ Describe situations which cause Alexander's followers to doubt him.

○ List some events in the story which demonstrated Alexander's respect and compassion for life.

LEVEL 3 (APPLICATION)

○ Compare Alexander's feats with a modern day conqueror.

○ How was Alexander's childhood different from yours? Explain.

72

○ Which part of the world, conquered by Alexander, would you like to visit with your parents? Why?

○ Do you think it is possible for someone to do what Alexander did in today's world? If so, why?

LEVEL 4 (ANALYSIS)

○ Compare Alexander to other famous men in history.

○ Which events in the story would it have been better for Alexander to avoid?

○ Analyze Alexander's personality.

○ Who had a bigger influence on Alexander, his mother or his father?

LEVEL 5 (SYNTHESIS)

○ If Alexander had lived a full life where else might he have gone to acquire new territory?

○ Make up some positive things Alexander did in his life which were not included in the story.

○ Describe Alexander and his accomplishments in a positive viewpoint. Describe Alexander and his accomplishments in a negative viewpoint.

○ If Alexander lived another 25 years, what other things might he have accomplished?

LEVEL 6 (EVALUATION)

○ Which of Alexander's personal qualities could be classified as negative?

○ Which event in the story should Alexander have most definitely avoided?

○ In today's world which professions would be appropriate for someone like Alexander?

○ How did Alexander contribute to humankind?

"B" Is For Betsy

by Carolyn Haywood

The adventures of a young girl named Betsy. A shared friendship, surprises, and kindness to the very end.

LEVEL 1 (KNOWLEDGE)

o What did Betsy's mother put in her book bag on the first day of school?

o Who was Betsy's best friend?

o What did Betsy want to give Ellen for her birthday?

o What was Betsy's dog's name?

LEVEL 2 (COMPREHENSION)

o Describe how Wiggle and Waggle grew up.

o Explain who Grandma Pretzie was.

o Describe how the circus came to Miss Grey's class.

o Explain how Betsy received her pet dog.

LEVEL 3 (APPLICATION)

o How does your school compare to Betsy's school?

o Who do you know that is like Grandma Pretzie or Mr. Kilpatrick? Explain.

o What children in your class would love to be in a circus? Name them and tell who they would like to be in a circus.

o Compare your best friend with Betsy's best friend Ellen.

LEVEL 4 (ANALYSIS)

o Describe your favorite part of the story. Be specific.

o Compare Miss Grey to your teacher.

o Explain why Mr. Applebee gave Betsy a puppy.

o Which event in the story would you like to change? Why?

LEVEL 5 (SYNTHESIS)

o Suppose Miss Grey wasn't a nice person. How would this have changed the story?

o Think of other things Betsy and Ellen might have done in their story. Describe them.

o If you were Betsy's friend, what would you want to tell her? Be specific.

o How would this story be different if it were to have taken place in another country? Perhaps an unfriendly country.

LEVEL 6 (EVALUATION)

o Describe the events in the story which made you very happy.

o Describe what type of person Miss Grey was in the story.

o Predict what will happen to the relationship between Betsy and Ellen?

o What stories have you heard or what experiences have you had similar to Betsy's story? Describe them.

The Purple Coat

by Amy Hest

Every fall, when the leaves start melting into autumn shades, Mama says, "Coat time, Gabrielle," and they ride two trains to Grampa's tailor shop in the city. Every year it's the same trip, every year the same coat—navy blue, plain. This year, there's bound to be trouble, for Gabby wants a purple coat.

LEVEL 1 (KNOWLEDGE)

○ Where did Grampa have his tailor shop?

○ How did Gabrielle and Mama get to Grampa's tailor shop?

○ What different kind of coat did Mama ask for when she was little?

○ What kind of coat did Grampa make for Gabrielle?

LEVEL 2 (COMPREHENSION)

○ Describe what Grampa always made for Gabrielle.

○ Describe how Gabrielle and Mama got to Grampa's shop.

○ Explain why Mama and Grampa always wanted Gabrielle to have a blue coat.

○ Tell what kind of coat Grampa made for Gabrielle.

LEVEL 3 (APPLICATION)

○ If you were Gabrielle, what type of coat would you want? Describe it?

○ What do you visit the big city for? Explain.

○ Did your Grampa ever made anything for you? Explain.

○ What did you like about Gabrielle's new coat?

LEVEL 4 (ANALYSIS)

○ Compare Gabrielle's new coat to one of your coats.

○ What type of person was Grampa?

○ Why did Mama always want Gabrielle to have a blue coat?

○ Why did Grampa make the new coat reversible?

LEVEL 5 (SYNTHESIS)

○ If you were Grampa, what kind of coat would you make for Gabrielle?

○ Instead of coats, suppose Grampa was a shoe maker, what kind of shoes would Gabrielle want?

○ Think of a few different kinds of coats Grampa could make in his shop.

○ Who else does Grampa make coats for?

LEVEL 6 (EVALUATION)

○ Do you think Gabrielle was right in asking for a purple coat? Why?

○ Evaluate Grampa as a coat maker.

○ How much did it cost to visit Grampa in New York City?

○ Predict what kind of coat Gabrielle will want next year.

Aldo Ice Cream

by Johanna Hurwitz

Aldo starts his ninth summer with modest ambitions—but when Mrs. Sossi asks him to help her deliver Meals on Wheels to the elderly and housebound, Aldo becomes unexpectedly busy. Finding ways to fill their empty days challenges his ingenuity, but the real challenge develops when Aldo decides to buy his sister the ice-cream maker she wants for her birthday.

LEVEL 1 (KNOWLEDGE)

○ Who was Aldo's best friend?

○ What were Aldo's sisters' names?

○ Which elderly person did Aldo like to visit?

○ For whom did Aldo want to buy the ice cream machine?

○ What kind of a contest did Aldo win?

LEVEL 2 (COMPREHENSION)

○ Describe how Aldo helped his mom with the Meals on Wheels program.

○ Describe what Aldo did while his best friend De De was away.

○ Explain how Aldo won the Grubby Sneaker Contest.

○ Tell what made buying the ice cream maker possible.

LEVEL 3 (APPLICATION)

○ Have you ever done community service like Aldo did in the story? Explain.

- What types of programs do you have for the elderly in your neighborhood? Describe them.

- Tell about your favorite ice cream flavor.

- How would you like to have an ice cream maker?

LEVEL 4 (ANALYSIS)

- Name the event in the story which demonstrated what kind of boy Aldo was.

- Compare what Aldo did for his sister to something you have done for your brother or sister.

- Identify an event in the story that has happened to you.

- Identify ways in which Aldo is like your best friend.

LEVEL 5 (SYNTHESIS)

- Change the story and have Aldo acquire the money for his sister's ice cream maker in a different way.

- Name other ways Aldo could have raised the needed money.

- Suppose the new ice cream maker is a "Magical Ice Cream Maker." What would it be like?

- Think of some new ice cream flavors.

LEVEL 6 (EVALUATION)

- Judge Mrs. Sossi's character as an individual.

- Think about the last time you needed money—who needed it more? You or Aldo?

○ Predict what kind of person Aldo will be as an adult.

○ Predict what other types of programs they will have for the elderly in the future.

Busy Body Nora

by Johanna Hurwitz

A medium size apartment house, eight stories high, is the setting for this story cycle about a little girl growing up in New York City. A curious six-year-old, Nora, wants to know all about the two hundred people in her building, and so she asks what their names are at every opportunity. Now and then someone thinks that Nora is a busybody.

LEVEL 1 (KNOWLEDGE)

O What was Nora's little brother's name?

O Where did Nora and her family live?

O Which person in the story knew all the names of all the people who lived in the building?

O Who was given a great big party in the story?

LEVEL 2 (COMPREHENSION)

O Explain how Nora's mother made the Stone Soup.

O Explain how Nora became Peter's baby sitter one day.

O Tell why Nora and Peter were so fond of Mrs. Hettlebrand.

O Describe Dad's special birthday party.

LEVEL 3 (APPLICATION)

O Why were the people who lived in the apartment house so friendly to each other?

○ What would be the best thing about living in a big apartment house in the city?

○ Do you know someone who lives in a big apartment house. Tell about him or her.

○ Is it possible to become friendly with everyone in a big apartment house? If yes, why?

LEVEL 4 (ANALYSIS)

○ Analyze the relationship between Nora and Peter.

○ Why would it be difficult for Nora to move to the country?

○ Is it necessary for a doorman to be friendly? Why?

○ Do people who live in apartment houses know the business and interests of all the other people in the building? Explain.

LEVEL 5 (SYNTHESIS)

○ If you were to move into a big apartment house next week what concerns would you have right now?

○ Who would you want to move with you if your family were to move into a large apartment house? Name them.

○ Tell about a funny thing that could happen to someone living in a big apartment house.

○ As Nora grows up, describe different things she will get involved in while living in her apartment house.

LEVEL 6 (EVALUATION)

○ What's great about living in a big apartment house?

○ What's not so great about living in a big apartment house?

○ Judge whether Nora and her family were happy living together.

○ Predict whether Nora and her family will remain living in the apartment house in the future.

Class Clown

by Johanna Hurwitz

Lucas Cott is one of the smartest kids in Mrs. Hockaday's third grade, but he is also the most rambunctious. Lucas doesn't mean to be the class clown, so he promises to try to behave, even though it doesn't sound like much fun.

LEVEL 1 (KNOWLEDGE)

○ What word did Mrs. Hockaday use to describe Lucas' behavior?

○ Who was the brain that sat next to Lucas?

○ What did Lucas bring to class that caused Mrs. Hockaday to get angry?

○ What part did Lucas play in the class circus?

LEVEL 2 (COMPREHENSION)

○ Explain what Lucas did to his desk.

○ Describe what happened during the school assembly.

○ Describe what happened when Mrs. Cott took the children for a haircut.

○ Explain how Mrs. Hockaday felt about Lucas at the end of the school year.

LEVEL 3 (APPLICATION)

○ Do you know anyone who is a "class clown"? Describe this person.

○ What would you do if you saw Lucas writing his name into the desk?

○ What problems can a class clown cause? Name them.

○ How would your teacher react to Lucas?

LEVEL 4 (ANALYSIS)

○ Compare Lucas to a class clown that you know.

○ Compare Mrs. Hockaday to a teacher you know.

○ Why does Lucas always fool around in school?

○ Name the event in the story which really shows Lucas's personality.

LEVEL 5 (SYNTHESIS)

○ Suppose Lucas's teacher was the meanest teacher in the world—what might happen?

○ Think of other things Lucas could do as class clown.

○ Suppose you were Lucas—explain to your mother exactly why you fool around so much.

○ Describe a "class clown" in your own words.

LEVEL 6 (EVALUATION)

○ Judge Mrs. Hockaday's handling of Lucas.

○ Predict what Lucas will be like as an adult.

○ Does every class have a "class clown"? Explain.

○ What kinds of jobs do class clowns get when they become adults?

Just So Stories—The Elephant Child

by Rudyard Kipling

An adventure of a highly curious young elephant who searches for a crocodile. When he finally meets the crocodile, his appearance changes as his nose is stretched and stretched and stretched!

LEVEL 1 (KNOWLEDGE)

○ Name the Elephant Child's family members.

○ What questions did he ask of his family?

○ How did his family react to his curiosity and questions?

○ Who told the Elephant where to find the crocodile?

LEVEL 2 (COMPREHENSION)

○ Describe what the Elephant Child took on his trip.

○ Describe what the Limpopo River looked like.

○ Explain how the Bi-Coloured-Python-Rock Snake helped the Elephant Child.

○ What new skills or abilities did the Elephant Child develop after his nose was stretched? Be specific.

LEVEL 3 (APPLICATION)

○ Describe things that could happen to an overly curious person.

○ How would your family react to you if you were as curious as the Elephant Child?

○ Name some other animals that might have had their features changed as a result of being highly curious.

○ Relate how you would have felt if you were the Elephant Child.

LEVEL 4 (ANALYSIS)

○ What parts of the story made you feel sorry for the Elephant Child?

○ Analyze the Elephant Child's thoughts after discovering his new abilities.

○ Which character in the story would you most like to be? Why?

○ Identify an event in the story which made you realize what kind of animal the Elephant Child was.

LEVEL 5 (SYNTHESIS)

○ Think of ways the Elephant Child could have avoided the Crocodile.

○ What might have happened had the snake not been able to help the Elephant Child?

○ Suppose the Elephant Child's family accepted him. How might the story be different?

○ Name some other types of animals who could have stretched the Elephant Child's nose.

LEVEL 6 (EVALUATION)

○ How would you describe the Bi-Coloured-Python-Rock Snake? What was his personality like?

○ List other things the Elephant's trunk enables him to do.

○ What will the Elephant Child's curiosity be like in the future?

○ How would you change this story? What would you make different in the story? Explain. Be specific.

Just So Stories—How The Camel Got His Hump

by Rudyard Kipling

"Djinn of All Deserts" listens to the complaints from a Horse, a Dog, and an Ox describing the laziness of a certain Camel. Using his magical powers, Djinn creates a HUMP on the Camel,s back and sets him off to explore his new self.

LEVEL 1 (KNOWLEDGE)

○ What three animals ask the Camel for help?

○ What types of job did the animals need help with?

○ What expression did the Camel use when refusing to help his animal friends?

○ How did the Dijinn create the hump on the Camel's back?

LEVEL 2 (COMPREHENSION)

○ Describe how each animal appeared in the story. What did each have that was different?

○ Describe what the Camel was chewing.

○ Explain how the Djinn appeared to the animals.

○ Describe how the Djinn used his magic in making the hump.

LEVEL 3 (APPLICATION)

○ Who does the lazy Camel remind you of in your real life?

○ How are Camels used today? For what purposes?

○ What other animals would you classify as lazy?

○ Why are Camels found mostly on the desert?

LEVEL 4 (ANALYSIS)

○ Identify the parts of the story where the animals became angry with the camel.

○ What job would the Camel have been most suited for—providing he was willing to work?

○ How would you physically compare the Camel with the horse and the ox?

○ Identify the event in the story which made you aware of what might happen to the Camel.

LEVEL 5 (SYNTHESIS)

○ Imagine what else the Dijinn could have done to the Camel.

○ What if there wasn't a "Dijinn of the Desert"? How might the animals have dealt with the lazy Camel?

○ Create a different ending to the story.

○ What other animals might the Dijinn have given new features to?

LEVEL 6 (EVALUATION)

○ Should the animals have asked the Camel for help? If yes, why?

○ How would you like it if someone were to put a hump on your back just for being lazy?

○ What would happen if all animals "did nothing"?

○ What did the Dijinn give the Camel that was positive? Explain.

Jason and the Money Tree

by Sona Levitin

Jason Galloway was too old to believe in magic, and he knew no tree would produce ten dollar bills. But that's exactly what was happening in his own backyard!

LEVEL 1 (KNOWLEDGE)

o Who gave Jason his money tree?

o Where did he keep his money tree?

o What did the money tree produce?

o To whom did Jason eventually give his money?

LEVEL 2 (COMPREHENSION)

o Describe how money grew on Jason's money tree.

o Explain what happened to some of the money tree buds.

o Describe some of Jason's "fears" about acquiring "free" money.

o Describe what happened to the money tree.

LEVEL 3 (APPLICATION)

o How would you have kept a money tree healthy and productive?

o What would you have done with your first ten dollar bill?

o Whom could you tell about your secret money tree? Why could you tell that person?

o If you had a rich money tree, what people in life would you want to help?

LEVEL 4 (ANALYSIS)

o Compare Jason's attitude about acquiring "free" money to what your attitude might be.

o Where would you have kept your money tree? Explain.

o Describe other ways a person could get "free" money.

o Analyze Jason's fears about people finding out about his money tree.

LEVEL 5 (SYNTHESIS)

o Describe what would have happened if Jason's money tree had produced thousands and thousands of dollars.

o List what you would do if you had a secret money tree which produced a million dollars.

o Create a new ending to the story.

o Describe ways to build a money tree and have it give you "free" money.

LEVEL 6 (EVALUATION)

o Predict what might have happened if Jason's money tree kept producing ten dollar bills.

o Judge the ways Jason kept his money tree a secret.

o If Jason's money tree produced a million dollars, what would happen to the money if it were discovered by the police.

o Which event in the story would you like to change? Why?

Pippi Longstocking

by Astrid Lindgren

A nine-year-old girl named Pippi Longstocking has the challenge and freedom of living alone and deciding what to do and how to do it! A spunky kid with a marvelous imagination!

LEVEL 1 (KNOWLEDGE)

○ Where did Pippi live?

○ Who were Pippi's young friends?

○ Name Pippi's two pets?

○ What did Pippi like to eat?

LEVEL 2 (COMPREHENSION)

○ Describe what a "thing-finder" is.

○ Describe Pippi's first day in school.

○ Explain why the audience liked and applauded Pippi at the circus.

○ Explain how Pippi became the town's favorite little person.

LEVEL 3 (APPLICATION)

○ Why would it be difficult to live as Pippi did?

○ If you were Pippi what other things would you have liked to do?

○ Who among the people you know reminds you of Pippi? How?

○ Would your parents like Pippi? Why?

LEVEL 4 (ANALYSIS)

○ Describe the relationship between Pippi, Annika, and Tommy.

○ Which event in the story did you find most enjoyable?

○ Why would Pippi have difficulty being in your class? Explain.

○ List several characteristics you would use in describing Pippi Longstocking.

LEVEL 5 (SYNTHESIS)

○ Suppose Pippi was not allowed to live alone. How would it have changed her lifestyle?

○ Make up some new situations Pippi and her friends could experience in the story.

○ What kinds of questions would your parents ask Pippi if she visited your house?

○ Describe Pippi as an adult.

LEVEL 6 (EVALUATION)

○ Describe what you like about Pippi. Be specific.

○ Why would it be impossible for Pippi to live alone?

○ What things does this story teach us about young children?

○ Choose the three things you like about Pippi's life.

Mrs. Piggle-Wiggle's Magic

by Betty MacDonald

The story is about Mrs. Piggle-Wiggle's magical cures. Several parents call Mrs. Piggle-Wiggles and each is given a special cure for the various problems they are experiencing with their children.

LEVEL 1 (KNOWLEDGE)

o Name the different cures used by Mrs. Piggle-Wiggles.

o Describe Lester the pig. What was he like?

o What cure was used with the Interrupters?

o What did Mrs. Piggle-Wiggles find at the end of the story?

LEVEL 2 (COMPREHENSION)

o Explain how Lester got Christopher to improve in his table manners.

o Describe the change in Jody's behavior. What made her now want to go to school?

o What were some of the things Sharon broke during her heedless breaking moments?

o Describe what the tattletale cure looked like.

LEVEL 3 (APPLICATION)

o What cures might your parents request from Mrs. Piggle-Wiggles?

o What cures do you know about that are used by parents?

o How would your parents feel about giving you a special powder or pill or animal?

o Should there be cures for parents to use?

LEVEL 4 (ANALYSIS)

o Describe which cure parents would use the most. The least.

o Identify the things which make Mrs. Piggle-Wiggles a nice person.

o Compare one of Mrs. Piggle-Wiggles cures to something your parents might use to change behavior.

o Identify a person in the story who most resembles you. How?

LEVEL 5 (SYNTHESIS)

o Think of other cures Mrs. Piggle-Wiggles could give the parents.

o Suppose the cure was forever. Which cure in the story would cause someone a real problem?

o Suppose the children went to Mrs. Piggle-Wiggles for cures to use on their parents. What parent behavior would they need to cure?

o Describe what a "Cure" store would look like.

LEVEL 6 (EVALUATION)

o Do you think "Cures" are necessary for using with children?

o Decide which "Cure" all parents should have.

o Why might "Cures" be dangerous?

o Do you think there are people like Mrs. Piggle-Wiggles? If so, explain.

Miss Pickerell On The Trail

Ellen MacGregor and Dora Pantell

No one, not even the Governor or Professor Humwhistel, the famous space detective, knows what is causing the mysterious attack on the western side of Square Toe Mountain. Miss Pickerell resolutely puts the clues together and gets on the trail to solve the problem.

LEVEL 1 (KNOWLEDGE)

○ Who was Miss Pickerell's nephew?

○ Where did Miss Pickerell live?

○ What were the names of Miss Pickerell's two pets?

○ What caused the acid rain problem on Square Toe Mountain?

○ How did Miss Pickerell find the problem?

LEVEL 2 (COMPREHENSION)

○ Describe the problem at Square Toe Mountain.

○ Explain how Euphus discovered the acid problem.

○ Explain how Miss Pickerell and the Governor met Mr. Flintstone.

○ Tell how the President helped solve the problem.

LEVEL 3 (APPLICATION)

○ Have you ever heard about or experienced a pollution problem where you live? If so, tell about it.

o What other problems could result from air pollution?

o Who protects our environment from pollution?

o How can we stop pollution?

LEVEL 4 (ANALYSIS)

o How did Miss Pickerell know it was the smoke stacks causing the acid problem?

o How would you compare Miss Pickerell's acid problem to a problem in your community?

o Why would businesses pollute the air? Explain.

o What type of boy was Euphus?

LEVEL 5 (SYNTHESIS)

o What if the President and the State Senator refused to help with the acid problem? What would Miss Pickerell and the Governor do?

o Suppose Mr. Flintstone captured Miss Pickerell, the Governor, Euphus, and the others and refused to let them go. What might have happened?

o Pretend you were with Euphus on the search. What thoughts would you have had in discovering the big factory?

o Change the ending to the story. Create an entirely different ending.

LEVEL 6 (EVALUATION)

o Judge whether large factories could pollute the air and water?

o Why would it be difficult for Miss Pickerell to talk to the President of the United States?

o Predict how long it will take before the problem is solved on Square Toe Mountain.

o Predict what Euphus will be when he grows up.

Sarah, Plain and Tall

by Patricia MacLachlan

Caleb doesn't remember Mama, who died a day after he was born. But his other sister, Anna, says Papa and Mama sang "every single day." Now Papa doesn't sing at all. Papa places an ad in the newspaper for a wife and he receives an answer from a woman named Sarah. Sarah writes, "I will come by train..." and the beautiful story begins!

LEVEL 1 (KNOWLEDGE)

o How did Papa contact Sarah?

o Where did Sarah come from?

o What did Papa teach Sarah to do?

o What were Sarah's favorite colors?

o What did Sarah miss after she came to live with Papa?

LEVEL 2 (COMPREHENSION)

o Describe what Papa and the children liked to do.

o Describe what Sarah looked like when she arrived at the farm.

o Tell what Sarah liked to do during the day.

o Why did the children think that Sarah might not return from her trip into town?

LEVEL 3 (APPLICATION)

o Do you know any boys and girls who have new moms?

○ How is Sarah like your mom?

○ Would your papa place an ad in the newspaper for a new wife if he found himself in a similar situation as Mr. Jacob Witting was in?

○ Why would it be difficult to get to know and like a new mom?

LEVEL 4 (ANALYSIS)

○ Analyze the things the family did for recreation.

○ Compare Mr. Witting to your dad or uncle.

○ Compare your home to the Witting home.

○ Analyze Sarah's personality.

LEVEL 5 (SYNTHESIS)

○ Think of other ways papa could have met a new wife.

○ Suppose Sarah was unfriendly. How would the family have reacted.

○ How would this story be different if it had taken place in a large city?

○ Describe a vacation back to Maine. Tell what Sarah would do with her new family.

LEVEL 6 (EVALUATION)

○ Why would it be difficult to select a new wife?

○ Predict how Sarah and the family will get along in the future.

○ Evaluate the Witting family lifestyle.

○ Describe what you learned from this story.

Amelia Bedelia Helps Out

by Peggy Parish

Amelia Bedelia and her young friend Effie Lou visit Miss Emma and proceed to help her—only there's a communication problem resulting in some amusing situations.

LEVEL 1 (KNOWLEDGE)

○ Whose house did Amelia Bedelia and Effie Lou go to?

○ What was the first job given to Amelia Bedelia and Effie Lou?

○ What did Amelia Bedelia and Effie Lou do to the bean plants?

○ What kind of cake did Amelia Bedelia and Effie Lou make for Miss Emma?

LEVEL 2 (COMPREHENSION)

○ Describe what Amelia Bedelia and Effie Lou did to the garden.

○ Explain how the bean plants were staked.

○ Tell how Amelia Bedelia and Effie Lou attempted to fix the bare spot in Miss Emma's front lawn.

○ Tell about Miss Emma's reaction to what Amelia Bedelia and Effie Lou had done.

LEVEL 3 (APPLICATION)

○ Have you ever tried to help someone and made the situation worse?

○ Why did Amelia Bedelia and Effie Lou have so much trouble understanding Miss Emma?

○ How would you have weeded the garden?

○ How would you stake bean plants?

LEVEL 4 (ANALYSIS)

○ Why was there such confusion in interpreting what Miss Emma wanted done?

○ What does Amelia Bedelia need to do in the future when helping someone?

○ Analyze Miss Emma's reaction to what Amelia Bedelia and Effie Lou had done.

○ Compare something Amelia Bedelia did in the story to something you messed up in trying to be helpful to someone.

LEVEL 5 (SYNTHESIS)

○ Think of other jobs Miss Emma could have given Amelia Bedelia—only to be messed up.

○ Think of a new title for this story.

○ What if Amelia Bedelia and Effie Lou had been paid for their work? What might have happened?

○ What will the next situation be like when Amelia Bedelia and Effie Lou volunteer to help Miss Emma?

LEVEL 6 (EVALUATION)

○ Are there other terms or phrases which have multiple meanings? Explain.

○ Evaluate Amelia Bedelia and Effie Lou's work effort.

○ Why won't Miss Emma ask Amelia Bedelia and Effie Lou to help her in the future?

○ Evaluate Miss Emma's choice of language when explaining what she wanted done.

Freaky Friday

by Mary Rodgers

A young girl named Annabel turns herself into her mother for a day. The mother becomes Annabel. Annabel, now the mother, must deal with a day filled with excitement and unexpected events.

LEVEL 1 (KNOWLEDGE)

○ What was Annabel's brother's nickname?

○ Name three situations Annabel had to deal with (while in her mother's body).

○ How old was Annabel in the story?

○ Who was the babysitter in the story?

LEVEL 2 (COMPREHENSION)

○ Why did Annabel fire the cleaning lady?

○ What did Annabel learn from her meeting with the school personnel?

○ Explain what Mr. Andrews wanted his wife (now Annabel) to do that day?

○ Describe Annabel's performance in school.

LEVEL 3 (APPLICATION)

○ Which parent would you like to become for a day? Why?

○ How does Mr. & Mrs. Andrews' daily activities compare to your parents' activities?

○ What things would you like to do if you became a parent for a day?

○ How is Annabel's relationship with her brother similar to your relationship with your brother or sister?

LEVEL 4 (ANALYSIS)

○ Why do you think Annabel wanted to become her mother for a day?

○ Describe which event was the most difficult for Annabel to deal with (as her mother).

○ Tell which part of the story you enjoyed most. Why?

○ Relate what you like about Annabel. Be specific.

LEVEL 5 (SYNTHESIS)

○ Suppose Annabel remained in her mother's body. What might have happened?

○ Create other experiences Annabel might have had to deal with on this special Friday.

○ Change the story by adding one or two new family members.

○ Discuss other role changes in life. What animals would you like to switch with for a day? Explain.

LEVEL 6 (EVALUATION)

○ Why would you want to change roles with your mother or father for a day?

○ Judge whether Annabel learned anything important about her mother that day. Be specific.

○ Predict what might happen if families were able to switch roles occasionally.

○ How many children would be willing to switch roles with a parent for a day? Explain.

The Magic Grove

by Mihail Sadoveanu

Miss Liza wanders into a Magical Grove and discovers seven tiny Manikins and a beautiful Princess. Miss Liza hears the wonderful tales of the Grove.

LEVEL 1 (KNOWLEDGE)

○ What was Miss Liza's pet's name?

○ What type of little people did Miss Liza find in the Grove?

○ Who were the Manikins carrying through the Grove?

○ What story did the Manikins tell Miss Liza?

LEVEL 2 (COMPREHENSION)

○ Describe the Grove when Miss Liza first discovered it.

○ Describe what the Manikins looked like.

○ Tell what Miss Liza's mother use to say about tales.

○ Explain how Miss Liza returned from the Magic Grove.

LEVEL 3 (APPLICATION)

○ Have you ever seen a beautiful grove? Explain.

○ Where else have you heard stories about seven little people and a Princess?

○ Do your parents tell you about tales from the past? Explain.

○ Are groves filled with little creatures at night? Explain.

LEVEL 4 (ANALYSIS)

○ Compare Miss Liza's fantasy with a dream fantasy you have had.

○ Analyze Miss Liza's thoughts when the Manikins appeared.

○ What will be Miss Liza's fondest memory from her experience in the Magic Grove?

○ Describe the relationship between Miss Lisa and Petra.

LEVEL 5 (SYNTHESIS)

○ Suppose the Manikins were mean little people. What might have happened to Miss Liza?

○ Create another tale about the Princess of the Magic Grove.

○ Tell about Miss Liza's next visit to the Magic Grove.

○ Describe how Miss Liza will tell her mother of the Magic Grove experience.

LEVEL 6 (EVALUATION)

○ Do you think Miss Liza will return to her Magic Grove fantasy? If yes, explain.

○ Why was it important that Miss Liza had Petra with her during the experience?

○ Evaluate Miss Liza's fantasy images of the Magic Grove.

○ Why are fantasy stories valuable for us to experience? Explain.

The Cricket In Times Square

by George Selden

The cricket—his name is Chester and he hails from Connecticut—spends only one summer in New York City; but he will never forget the adventures he has there with his three friends, a little boy named Mario, a fast-talking Broadway mouse named Tucker and his pal, Harry the Cat.

LEVEL 1 (KNOWLEDGE)

○ Where did Chester live?

○ Who became Chester's best friends?

○ How did Chester become famous?

○ Why did Chester return to Connecticut?

LEVEL 2 (COMPREHENSION)

○ Describe how Chester got his first meal in New York City.

○ Explain why Mario took Chester to Chinatown.

○ List the different songs Chester played.

○ Describe the relationship between Chester, Tucker, and Harry.

LEVEL 3 (APPLICATION)

○ How would your pet react to a cricket?

○ If you had a pet cricket, how would you take care of him?

○ How would you describe the sounds made by crickets?

o What would you give your pet cricket to eat?

LEVEL 4 (ANALYSIS)

o Compare living in a newsstand to living in someone's home (for Chester the Cricket).

o Which event in the story was most amusing? Explain.

o Why did Chester draw such large crowds while performing at the newsstand?

o Why didn't other crickets come to live at the newsstand?

LEVEL 5 (SYNTHESIS)

o Create one additional friend Chester finds while visiting New York City. Tell about this new friend.

o Suppose Mama made Mario get rid of Chester. How might he have accomplished it?

o Instead of a newsstand, describe the story taking place in another location in New York City.

o Select a favorite character in this story. Tell why you have selected this character.

LEVEL 6 (EVALUATION)

o Judge whether someone could have a pet cricket.

o Predict what might happen to Chester when he returns to Connecticut.

o Judge whether a cricket, a house, and a cat could be friendly to each other.

o Which event in the story was the most "unreal."

Into The Dream

by William Sleator

This imaginative story is about two children who experience the same strange dream. Each night their dream became more frightening and intense, until finally they discover a small child with an amazing ability of communicating without "words"..."ESP"..."Extra Sensory Perception."

LEVEL 1 (KNOWLEDGE)

○ Name the two children who experienced the same dream each night.

○ Who was the woman that experienced a UFO while in Nevada?

○ How did Paul and Francine discover Mrs. Jaleela?

○ From whom were Paul, Francine, Noah, and Cookie trying to escape in the story?

○ How was Paul saved at the end of the story?

LEVEL 2 (COMPREHENSION)

○ Describe Paul and Francine's dream.

○ Explain how they discovered Noah's special abilities.

○ Describe how the children and Cookie escaped from the two strange men.

○ Tell how Noah saved Paul's life.

LEVEL 3 (APPLICATION)

○ Have you ever experienced a dream like Paul and Francine's? If so, describe what it was like.

○ Where have you heard about the term (ESP) Extra Sensory Perception?

○ Why do some dreams reoccur? Explain.

○ Do any of your friends talk about dreams? If yes, in what ways? Explain.

LEVEL 4 (ANALYSIS)

○ Which event in the story led you to believe that it was science fiction?

○ Why did the two strange men in the story scare you?

○ Compare your worst dream with the dream experienced by Paul and Francine.

○ Tell about a time when you were thinking the same thing as someone in your family was thinking.

LEVEL 5 (SYNTHESIS)

○ Explain what it would be like if everybody had a "high" degree of Extra Sensory Perception.

○ Suppose the two strange men in the story captured Noah. What would they have done with him?

○ How does a dog communicate to another dog? Explain.

○ Continue the story. Suppose everyone saw the children on TV. What might happen to them in the future.

LEVEL 6 (EVALUATION)

○ What questions came to your mind as a result of reading the science fiction story?

o Are some people able to predict the future better than others? Explain.

o Do you think we should study more about ESP? If so, why?

o Who knows what your thinking sometimes? Mommy or daddy?

The Case of the Exploding Plumbing (From Encyclopedia Brown No. 11)

by Donald J. Sobol

Gladys smashed all Winslow's antiques in order to hide the fact that she was interested only in the lion. She also exploded Winslow's plumbing. Encyclopedia solves the case. Gladys was too greedy. She wanted to have the only lion to sell at the antique market.

LEVEL 1 (KNOWLEDGE)

o What was Winslow Brant known as in Idaville?

o What nearly killed Winslow?

o How old was Gladys Smith?

o What clue gave Encyclopedia the solution?

LEVEL 2 (COMPREHENSION)

o Describe what Gladys's station wagon looked like.

o Explain how Winslow's plumbing exploded.

o Why were Winslow's antiques in the basement?

o Describe what Encyclopedia found in the basement which was used to smash Winslow's antiques.

LEVEL 3 (APPLICATION)

o What do you have in your basement that you could sell?

o Have you ever seen a collection of antiques? Describe.

o How would you have felt if you were Winslow?

o What might he do with his antiques in the future? Explain.

LEVEL 4 (ANALYSIS)

o Analyze Gladys's motives for smashing Winslow's antiques.

o Compare Gladys's crime to a crime that happened in your community involving teenagers.

o Which is Winslow's worst problem—the smashed antiques or the plumbing that exploded?

o Why did Encyclopedia know it was Gladys? Explain.

LEVEL 5 (SYNTHESIS)

o How will Winslow replace his smashed antique collection?

o Suppose Gladys didn't come over to Winslow's house. Would she still have gotten caught?

o What other crimes did Gladys commit during her teenage years? Be specific.

o Describe Glady's reaction when she knew that Encyclopedia was called to investigate the case.

LEVEL 6 (EVALUATION)

o Judge whether Gladys will commit other crimes in her life.

o How will Gladys repay Winslow for his loss and damage?

o Why is a basement a bad place to keep valuable antiques?

o Predict whether Encyclopedia will get similar cases like this one in the future.

Encyclopedia Brown And The Case Of The Midnight Visitor

by Donald J. Sobol

The only way Bugs Meany's Tigers could hear anything good about themselves was to talk to one another. They were out to disgrace Encyclopedia Brown, Idaville's ten year old supersleuth. In this story Encyclopedia takes them all on and solves ten new cases.

LEVEL 1 (KNOWLEDGE)

○ Who was Encyclopedia's father?

○ Who became Encyclopedia's assistant?

○ Name the cases solved by Encyclopedia.

○ What was Encyclopedia's business called?

LEVEL 2 (COMPREHENSION)

○ Explain how Encyclopedia solved the case of the Hidden Penny.

○ Explain how Encyclopedia solved the case of the Painting Gerbils.

○ Describe the clue left by Mr. Butler in the case of the Midnight Visitor.

○ Describe what Stinky did to be disqualified in the case of the Fifty Mosquitoes.

LEVEL 3 (APPLICATION)

○ Could you have solved some of the cases in this story? Which ones?

○ Is it possible for a ten-year old to be as smart as Encyclopedia? Explain.

○ Can you relate a personal experience similar to one of the cases in the story? Explain.

○ How would your parents feel if you were Encyclopedia Brown? Explain.

LEVEL 4 (ANALYSIS)

○ Compare Encyclopedia Brown to a ten-year-old you know who has similar traits.

○ Why would it be difficult for a ten-year-old to have a detective agency? Explain.

○ What makes Encyclopedia Brown such a good detective? Explain.

○ Which was your favorite case in the book? Why?

LEVEL 5 (SYNTHESIS)

○ If you could recommend someone from your class as an assistant detective to help Encyclopedia, who would it be, and why did you select that person?

○ Suppose Bugs Meany kidnapped Encyclopedia. What would have happened? Explain.

○ Think of a new case for Encyclopedia Brown to solve. Describe the case.

○ Name some modern technology that could help Encyclopedia's detective agency.

LEVEL 6 (EVALUATION)

○ Judge why you would or would not want to be like Encyclopedia Brown. Be specific.

○ Predict what Encyclopedia Brown will be like in the future.

○ Which case was the easiest for Encyclopedia to solve? Why?

○ Which case was the most difficult case for Encyclopedia to solve? Why?

Mr. Pepper Stories

by Mark Taylor

First Mr. Pepper fixes his house. Then he plants a garden. And then he tries to make some money. But Mr. Pepper doesn't know how to do any of these things. He thinks he knows how. And he does what he thinks is right. But what he does is always wrong.

LEVEL 1 (KNOWLEDGE)

○ What does Mr. Pepper try to fix in his house?

○ What does he do wrong when trying to make a garden?

○ What does Mr. Pepper finally do to his house which pleases Mrs. Sunshine?

○ What does Mr. Pepper fail at while trying to make money?

LEVEL 2 (COMPREHENSION)

○ Describe how Mr. Pepper tries to fix his house. Be specific.

○ Explain what Mrs. Sunshine suggests that Mr. Pepper do about fixing his house.

○ Tell what happens to Mr. Pepper's garden.

○ Describe how Mr. Pepper finally makes money.

LEVEL 3 (APPLICATION)

○ Whom do you know who is like Mr. Pepper?

○ Do you have any "How To" books in your house? If so, who uses them and for what reasons?

○ What other things could Mr. Pepper do to make money?

○ What advice do you have for Mr. Pepper?

LEVEL 4 (ANALYSIS)

○ Compare Mr. Pepper to your dad or uncle.

○ Analyze Mr. Pepper's attitude about life.

○ Why do Mr. Pepper and Mrs. Sunshine have such a nice relationship?

○ Which event in the story was Mr. Pepper's biggest "goof"?

LEVEL 5 (SYNTHESIS)

○ Create another Mr. Pepper story. Tell what trouble he gets himself into.

○ Would Mr. Pepper be different if he was married? If so, how?

○ Suppose Mr. Pepper was your father or unlce. What things would you want to talk to him about?

○ Suppose Mr. Pepper became your teacher. Imagine what the class would be like. Describe it.

LEVEL 6 (EVALUATION)

○ Judge whether Mr. Pepper would make a good friend.

○ Predict what trouble Mr. Pepper will get himself into in the future.

○ What do you like best about Mr. Pepper? Explain.

○ Should Mr. Pepper and Mrs. Sunshine live together? If so, why?

All of a Kind Family

by Sydney Taylor

A beautiful story about a family who lived in the lower east side of New York City. The caring, cooperation, and love for one another is depicted throughout the story. Mama and Papa and their five daughters make the best of what they have.

LEVEL 1 (KNOWLEDGE)

○ Name the five daughters.

○ Who lost the library book?

○ Who was their favorite uncle?

○ Where did the family visit?

○ Who became the new member of the family?

LEVEL 2 (COMPREHENSION)

○ Describe how Sarah would have to pay for her lost library book.

○ Describe the surprise the children found at Papa's shop.

○ Explain Mama's dusting game.

○ Tell about Uncle Charlie's sad moment in life.

LEVEL 3 (APPLICATION)

○ What types of chores does your family have for you?

○ Would you like to be a part of a large family like the one in the story? Explain.

○ What is the most difficult thing about being in a large family and being poor?

○ How would the family be different if there was one brother and the rest sisters?

LEVEL 4 (ANALYSIS)

○ Compare what the girls had to do to help Mama in the story to what you do at home for your parents.

○ Why did Sarah feel so terrible about losing the library book?

○ Did the children have enough time to play and have fun?

○ Which event in the story demonstrated how close the family was to one another?

LEVEL 5 (SYNTHESIS)

○ Suppose Mama and Papa became very rich. How would the family change?

○ Describe what it would be like to be the oldest sister in the family.

○ Name some things the sisters would enjoy doing if they had lived in today's world.

○ What else could they have gotten Papa for his birthday?

LEVEL 6 (EVALUATION)

○ Judge whether the sisters got along with each other.

○ Judge whether the librarian was fair in her arrangement with Sarah.

○ Predict what the relationship among the sisters will be in their later life.

○ Decide whether Mama was a fair person.

The Flight Of
The Kite Merriweather

by Mildred Teal

James Supworth had an abiding love for kites. His great love was born on a breezy day in May in Chicago, Illinois, the Windy City. He was eight at the time. By the time he was grown, he had progressed from simple kites to box kites, tetrahedrals, Japanese war kites, and windmills with hummers. The story centers on his one great kite "Merriweather" (a group of five kites).

LEVEL 1 (KNOWLEDGE)

○ What were the two personal characteristics James Supworth had as a young man?

○ How old was James when he had his first kite experience?

○ What nickname was James given when he became an adult?

○ Where did the Merriweather finally land?

○ Who was James Supworth's best and long-time friend?

LEVEL 2 (COMPREHENSION)

○ Describe some of the items on James Supworth's shopping list prior to building the Merriweather.

○ Describe what it was like the day the Merriweather was launched.

○ Explain how James Supworth recorded his flying kite experience.

o Describe some of the difficulties James experienced during the flight of the Merriweather.

LEVEL 3 (APPLICATION)

o Describe your experience with kites.

o If you were the captain of the Merriweather, where would you have taken it?

o How would you compare the Merriweather with today's hot air balloons?

o Who would you want to take with you on a flying kite expedition?

LEVEL 4 (ANALYSIS)

o Analyze James Supworth's beliefs, attitudes, and motivation.

o Identify the event that was the most difficult for James to deal with during his flight.

o Identify how Bill Boyle was such a good friend.

o Analyze the Merriweather kite. Tell why it was such a good kite.

LEVEL 5 (SYNTHESIS)

o Imagine other situations that could have happened during the flight of the Merriweather.

o Suppose the Merriweather drifted out into the Atlantic Ocean. What do you suppose James would have done?

o Describe how you would have made the kite, Merriweather, different. Be specific.

o Design a trip around the world for the kite, Merriweather.

LEVEL 6 (EVALUATION)

○ Describe how James felt when he encountered the smoke during his flight.

○ Who do you know that is like James Supworth? Describe this person.

○ How would you have made the Merriweather a safer kite? Explain.

○ Choose the one event in the story that would be the most dangerous. Why?

Peter and the Troll Baby

by Jan Wahl

Peter and his family go on vacation. While staying at a wood cottage, Peter's baby sister, Susanna, is stolen by the Trolls.

LEVEL 1 (KNOWLEDGE)

○ What was Peter's baby sister's name?

○ How did Peter and his family get to the wood cottage?

○ When did Peter discover that Susanna was taken away by the Trolls.

○ What did Peter use to get Susanna back from the Trolls?

LEVEL 2 (COMPREHENSION)

○ Describe the wood cottage where Peter and his family were vacationing.

○ Tell about Peter's wish.

○ Describe where the Trolls lived.

○ Explain how Peter rescued Susanna from the Trolls.

LEVEL 3 (APPLICATION)

○ Have you ever been away in the woods and had scary thoughts? Describe them.

○ Why is it bad to wish something negative would happen to someone else?

○ Have you ever heard of a baby being stolen? When? Where?

○ What did you learn from his story?

LEVEL 4 (ANALYSIS)

○ Analyze Peter's feelings when Susanna was taken by the Trolls.

○ Analyze Peter's plan for rescuing Susanna.

○ After Susanna was rescued, how do you think Peter felt toward his baby sister?

○ Compare this story with a story you have heard about a baby being stolen.

LEVEL 5 (SYNTHESIS)

○ How else could Peter have rescued Susanna? Explain.

○ Tell about the life of a Troll.

○ What would you want to say to Peter right now?

○ Make up new Troll features. Tell about what your Troll looks like.

LEVEL 6 (EVALUATION)

○ Tell why it is wrong to wish bad thoughts on someone.

○ Evaluate Peter's actions in getting Susanna back.

○ Predict Peter's relationship with Susanna in the future.

○ List three things this story teaches us.

Charlotte's Web

by E. B. White

A young girl develops a special relationship with a pet pig. The pig, named Wilbur, meets a small spider named Charlotte. When Wilbur's owner considers getting rid of him, Charlotte creates a special message, "Some Pig" in her web. Wilbur is saved and becomes famous.

LEVEL 1 (KNOWLEDGE)

○ Who were the main characters?

○ What words appeared in Charlotte's Web?

○ Who rescued Charlotte's egg sac?

○ What did Wilbur receive at the County Fair?

LEVEL 2 (COMPREHENSION)

○ Why did Mr. Zuckerman want to get rid of Wilbur?

○ Explain how the miracle happened?

○ Describe the relationship between Wilbur and Charlotte.

○ Explain what happened to Charlotte's children.

LEVEL 3 (APPLICATION)

○ If you were Wilbur, how would you have thanked Charlotte for saving your life?

○ Describe how you would have tried to save Wilbur when Mr. Zuckerman was considering doing away with him.

LEVEL 4 (ANALYSIS)

○ Why did Charlotte want to save Wilbur's life?

○ How would you describe Templeton's personality?

○ List some friends of yours who are as kind and thoughtful as Charlotte.

○ Why did Mr. Zuckerman change his mind about getting rid of Wilbur?

LEVEL 5 (SYNTHESIS)

○ How else might Wilbur have been saved in the story?

○ Create other problems which Wilbur might have experienced while living in the barn.

○ Imagine another way Charlotte could have made Wilbur famous.

○ Suppose Charlotte didn't die. What might have happened with her children?

LEVEL 6 (EVALUATION)

○ Do you think it would be a good idea to have a pet spider? If so, why?

○ Which part of the story would you like to change? Why? How would you change it?

○ Who do you think was the most clever character in the story and why?

○ Judge which character in the story reminded you of yourself. Tell why.

Stuart Little

by E. B. White

When Mrs. Fredick C. Little's second son arrived, everybody noticed that he was not much bigger than a mouse. The truth of the matter was, the baby looked very much like a mouse in every way. The adventures of Stuart Little follows.

LEVEL 1 (KNOWLEDGE)

o How tall was Stuart Little?

o What house pet became Stuart's best friend?

o Name two things Stuart drove in the story.

o What young lady did Stuart write a letter to?

LEVEL 2 (COMPREHENSION)

o Describe how Stuart helped his family in the beginning of the story.

o Describe how Margelo saved Stuart's life.

o Explain what happened to Stuart when he sailed the wasp for Dr. Carey.

o Explain how Stuart tried to find Margalo.

LEVEL 3 (APPLICATION)

o If you were Stuart Little what things would you have like to do in the story?

o Do you think a mouse and a cat could be pet friends? If so, how?

○ If Stuart lived in your house, what things might be dangerous to him?

LEVEL 4 (ANALYSIS)

○ Compare Stuart's life with his brother George's life.

○ Analyze Stuart's thoughts as he heads north in search of Margalo.

○ Identify an event in the story that has happened to you.

○ Choose an event in the story that you would like to have happen to you. Why did you choose it?

LEVEL 5 (SYNTHESIS)

○ Suppose the little cat was mean and nasty. How would this have affected Stuart's life?

○ Create other exciting things which Stuart could have done in the story.

○ Describe an ending to the story where Stuart finds Margalo.

○ Suppose Stuart was a giant. How would the story have been different?

LEVEL 6 (EVALUATION)

○ How would you have protected Stuart from danger? Be specific.

○ Select three qualities that you liked about Stuart.

○ Which event in the story did you least enjoy? Why?

○ Predict whether Stuart will find Margalo. If yes, how will he do it?

The Velveteen Rabbit

by Margery Williams

When a child loves you for a long, long time, not just to play with, but REALLY loves you, then you become Real...so is the story of Velveteen, a toy rabbit that is really loved!

LEVEL 1 (KNOWLEDGE)

○ Who tells the Velveteen Rabbit about how to become real?

○ When did the Velveteen Rabbit become real?

○ Who did the Velveteen Rabbit meet during the summer days?

○ What did the Fairy Flower do for Velveteen Rabbit?

LEVEL 2 (COMPREHENSION)

○ Explain what the Skin Horse said to Velveteen Rabbit about becoming Real.

○ Describe how the boy treated Velveteen Rabbit—thus making him Real.

○ What happened to Velveteen Rabbit when he became very anxious? Describe.

○ Explain what the Fairy Flower did for Velveteen Rabbit.

LEVEL 3 (APPLICATION)

○ Which toy of yours is almost "Real"? Tell about it.

○ How do your parents feel about the pet animals you really love? Explain.

○ Describe your favorite pet animal—either a favorite now or one you had when you were younger. Be specific.

○ Why should young children have pet animals?

LEVEL 4 (ANALYSIS)

○ Why did Skin Horse say it is not easy being Real?

○ Which things did the boy do to make the Velveteen Rabbit become Real?

○ How did the real rabbits know Velveteen was only a toy pet rabbit?

○ What did the boy do which really demonstrated his love for Velveteen Rabbit?

LEVEL 5 (SYNTHESIS)

○ How is your love for a pet animal different from your love of a real live pet animal? Explain.

○ Suppose children were not allowed to have any toy pet animals. What would it be like? How would the children feel?

○ How would you go about showing your toy pet animal how much you loved it? Explain.

○ What would a museum of toy pet animals be like? Describe it in detail.

LEVEL 6 (EVALUATION)

○ Predict whether children will always have toy pet animals.

○ What is the nicest thing about having a toy pet animal? Explain.

○ Why do grown-ups give up their love for toy pet animals?

○ Judge whether children should have more or less toy pet animals.

APPENDIX 1
Bloom's Taxonomy of Educational Objectives

KNOWLEDGE	SKILLS
1. Knowledge of specifics	*define, recognize*
knowledge of terminology	*recall*
knowledge of specific facts	*identify, label*
2. Knowledge of Ways of Dealing With Specifics	*understand*
knowledge of conventions	*examine*
knowledge of trends and sequences	*show*
knowledge of classifications and categories	*collect*
knowledge of criteria	
knowledge of methodology	
3. Knowledge of Universals & Abstractions in a Field	
knowledge of principles and generalizations	
knowledge of theories and structures	

COMPREHENSION

1. Translation	*translate, interpret*
2. Interpretation	*predict, summarize*
3. Extrapolation	*describe, explain*

APPLICATION — *apply, solve*

1. Use Abstractions in Specific & Concrete Situations	*experiment, show*

ANALYSIS — *connect, classify*

1. Analysis of Elements	*differentiate, relate*
2. Analysis of Relationships	*classify, arrange*
3. Analysis of Organizational Principles	*group, compare*

SYNTHESIS — *imagine*

1. Production of a Unique Communication	*design, redesign*
2. Production of a Plan for Operation	*combine, compose*
3. Derivation of a Set of Abstract Relations	*construct, translate*

EVALUATION

1. Judgments in Terms of Internal Evidence.	*interpret, judge*
2. Judgments in Terms of External Evidence.	*criticize, decide*

APPENDIX II

Verbs for Curriculum Development

Identification	Processes		
Model	Verb Delineation		
Taxonomy			
Knowledge	explain	relate	design
	show	code	interpret
Comprehension	list	take apart	judge
	observe	fill in	justify
Application	demonstrate	analyze	criticize
	uncover	take away	solve
Analysis	recognize	put together	decide
	discover	combine	
Synthesis	experiment	imagine	
	organize	suppose	
Evaluation	group	compare	
	collect	contrast	
	apply	add to	
	summarize	predict	
	order	assume	
	classify	translate	
	model	extend	
	construct	hypothesize	

Explanation: These verbs, randomly arranged beside the Taxonomy Model, are representative of the processes exemplified by the model.

APPENDIX III

What Happens to Students When Longer Wait-Times Occur?

1. The length of student responses increases. Explanatory statements increase from 400-800 percent.

2. The number of unsolicited but appropriate responses increases

3. Failure to respond decreases.

4. Confidence of children increases.

5. The incidence of speculative, creative thinking increases.

6. Teacher-centered teaching decreases, and student-centered interaction increases.

7. Students give more evidence before and after inference statements.

8. The number of questions asked by students increases.

9. The number of activities proposed by children increases.

10. Slow students contribute more: From 1.5 to 37 percent.

11. The variety of types of responses increases

12. Discipline problems decrease.

References

Aardema, Verna. *Why Mosquitoes Buzz In People's Ears*. New York: The Dial Press, 1975.

Atwater, Richard and Florence. *Mr. Popper's Penguins*. Boston: Little, Brown & Company, 1938.

Blume, Judy. *Blubber*. New York: Bradbury Press, 1974.

Blume, Judy. *Freckle Juice*. New York: Four Winds Press, 1971.

Blume, Judy. *Otherwise Known As Sheila The Great*. New York: Dutton, 1972.

Blume, Judy. *Superfudge*. New York: Dutton, 1980.

Blume, Judy. *Tales Of A Fourth Grade Nothing*. New York: Dutton, 1972.

Byars, Betsy. *The Computer Nut*, Betsy Byars. New York: Viking Press, 1984.

Byars, Betsy. *The 18th Emergency*. New York: The Viking Press, 1973.

Byars, Betsy. *The Pinballs*. New York: Apple Paperbacks, Scholastic, Inc., 1977.

Byars, Betsy. *The TV Kid*. New York: Apple Paperbacks, Scholastic, Inc., 1976.

Cleary, Beverly. *Ramona The Brave*. New York: William Morrow and Company, 1975.

Coontz, Otto. *Hornswoggle Magic*. Boston: Little, Brown and Company, 1981.

Dahl, Roald. *Charlie And The Chocolate Factory*. New York: Alfred Knopf, 1964.

Dahl, Roald. *George's Marvelous Medicine*. New York: A Bantam Skylane Book, 1982.

Dahl, Roald. *James And The Giant Peach*. New York: Alfred A. Knopf, 1961.

Embry, Margaret. *The Blue-Nosed Witch*. New York: A Bantam Skylark Book, 1956.

Estes, Eleanor. *The Hundred Dresses*. New York: Harcourt, Brace & World, Inc., 1944.

Evans, Mari. *JD*. Garden City, New York: Doubleday & Company, Inc., 1973.

Fleischman, Sid. *McBroom Tells The Truth*. New York: W. W. Norton & Company, Inc., 1966.

Fleming, Ian. *Chitty Chitty Bang Bang*. New York: Random House, 1964.

Graeber, Charlotte. *Mustard*. New York: MacMillan Publishing Company, Inc. 1982.

Greer, Gery and Bob Ruddick. *Max And Me And The Time Machine*. New York: Harcourt Brace Jovanovich Publishers, 1983.

Gunther, John. *Alexander The Great*. New York: Random House, 1953.

Haywood, Carolyn. *"B" Is For Betsy*. New York: Harcourt, Brace & World, Inc., 1939.

Hest, Amy. *The Purple Coat*. New York: Four Winds Press, 1986.

Hurwitz, Johanna. *Aldo Ice Cream*. New York: William Morrow and Company, 1981.

Hurwitz, Johanna. *Busy Body Nora*. New York: William Morrow and Company, 1976.

Hurwitz, Johanna. *Class Clown*. New York: William Morrow and Company, Inc., 1987.

Kipling, Rudyard. *The Elephant Child* (in *The Just So Stories*). New York: Doubleday & Company, 1902.

Kipling, Rudyard. *How The Camel Got His Hump* (in *The Just So Stories*). New York: Doubleday & Company, Inc, 1902.

Levitin, Sona. *Jason And The Money Tree*. New York: Harcourt Brace Jovanovich, 1974.

Lindgren, Astrid. *Pippi Longstocking*. New York: The Viking Press, 1950.

MacDonald, Betty. *Mrs. Piggle-Wiggle's Magic*. New York: Lippincott Jr. Books, 1952.

MacGregor, Ellen and Pantell, Dora. *Miss Pickerell On The Trail*. New York: McGraw Hill Book Company, 1982.

MacLachlan, Patricia. *Sarah, Plain And Tall*. New York: Harper & Row Publishers, 1985.

Parish, Peggy. *Amelia Bedelia Helps Out*. New York: Avon Books, 1979.

Rogers, Mary. *Freaky Friday*. New York: Harper & Row Publishers, 1972.

Sadoveanu, Mihail. *The Magic Grove*. London: Roydon Publishing Company, 1981.

Selden, George. *The Cricket In Times Square*. Mew York: Ariel Books, Farrar, Straus and Giroux, 1960.

Sleator, William*Into The Dream*. New York: E. P. Dutton, 1979.

Sobol, Donald J. *The Case Of The Exploding Plumbing*. New York: Scholastic Book Services, 1974.

Sobol, Donald J. *Encyclopedia Brown: And The Case Of The Midnight Visitor*. New York: Lodestar Books (E. P. Dutton), 1977.

Taylor, Mark. *Mr. Pepper Stories*. New York: Atheneum, 1984.

Taylor, Sydney. *All Of A Kind Family*. New York: Follett Publishing Company, 1951.

Teal, Mildred. *The Flight Of The Kite Merriweather*. New York: The Murray Printing Company, 1968.

Wahl, Jan.*Peter And The Troll Baby*. New York: A Golden Book, 1984.

White. E. B. *Charlotte's Web,*. New York: Harper & Row Jr. Books, 1952.

White, E. B. *Stuart Little*. New York: Harper & Row Jr. Books, 1945.

Williams, Margery. *The Velveteen Rabbit*. Garden City, New York: Doubleday & Company, Inc., 1965.